Robert Barnard

Robert Barnard was born and brought up in Essex. After reading English at Balliol College, Oxford, he worked for a time for the Fabian Society, and in 1961 went as a lecturer in English to the University of New England, in New South Wales. He taught in Norwegian universities for seventeen years from 1966, and in 1983 came back to Britain to write full time. As well as nearly thirty mysteries, he has written books on Dickens, Agatha Christie and a history of English literature. He and his wife now live in Leeds.

D0842009

By the same author

THE HABIT OF WIDOWHOOD
THE BAD SAMARITAN
MASTERS OF THE HOUSE
A HOVERING OF VULTURES
A FATAL ATTACHMENT
A SCANDAL IN BELGRAVIA
A CITY OF STRANGERS
DEATH AND THE CHASTE APPRENTICE
DEATH OF A SALESPERSON
AT DEATH'S DOOR
THE SKELETON IN THE GRASS
DEATH IN PURPLE PROSE
THE DISPOSAL OF THE LIVING
OUT OF THE BLACKOUT
A CORPSE IN A GILDED CAGE
LITTLE VICTIMS
MOTHER'S BOYS
DEATH IN A COLD CLIMATE
POSTHUMOUS PAPERS
UNRULY SON
DEATH ON THE HIGH C'S
BLOOD BROTHERHOOD
A LITTLE LOCAL MURDER
DEATH OF AN OLD GOAT

Perry Trethowan novels
BODIES
THE MISSING BRONTE
DEATH AND THE PRINCESS
SHEER TORTURE

ROBERT BARNARD

NO PLACE
OF SAFETY

HarperCollins*Publishers*

This novel is entirely a work of fiction.
The names, characters and incidents portrayed in it are
the work of the author's imagination. Any resemblance to
actual persons, living or dead, events or localities is
entirely coincidental.

HarperCollins*Publishers*
77–85 Fulham Palace Road,
Hammersmith, London W6 8JB

This paperback edition 1998
1 3 5 7 9 8 6 4 2

First published in Great Britain by
HarperCollins*Publishers* 1997

Copyright © Robert Barnard 1997

Robert Barnard asserts the moral right to
be identified as the author of this work

ISBN 0 00 649984 8

Printed and bound in Great Britain by
Clays Ltd, St Ives Plc

All rights reserved. No part of this publication may be
reproduced, stored in a retrieval system, or transmitted,
in any form or by any means, electronic, mechanical,
photocopying, recording or otherwise, without the prior
permission of the publishers.

This book is sold subject to the condition that it shall not,
by way of trade or otherwise, be lent, re-sold, hired out or
otherwise circulated without the publisher's prior consent
in any form of binding or cover other than that in which it
is published and without a similar condition including this
condition being imposed on the subsequent purchaser.

NO PLACE
OF SAFETY

CHAPTER 1

Missing Persons

Charlie Peace spotted the man he had come to talk to before he even got to number seventeen. It must have been policeman's instinct, or experience of parents whose children have suddenly left home. The man was approaching down the dingy street of terraced houses from the opposite direction. He was in his early fifties, and had a slightly dog-eared look: his shoulders were stooped, his moustache droopy and unkempt, the thin head of hair was uncombed. He was carrying a copy of the *Sun*. He looked the sort of man the world has not been kind to, and one who has not had the drive or personality to carve his own way in spite of it.

Sure enough he turned into number seventeen.

'Mr Coughlan?'

The man turned and looked at him, his hand still holding the key to open the front door. Charlie waved his ID card close to his eyes, which were bleared. When he had scanned it, the slack face registered surprise.

'Oh, I didn't expect –'

'A black copper?' said Charlie genially. 'Quite a lot of us around these days.'

The face appeared aggrieved.

'I didn't mean that. You're taking me up all wrong. I meant I didn't expect anyone from the police to come around. Ronnie Withers down at the Railway Arms said the police never bothered with missing teenagers. Said there were too many of them, and there was nothing they could do.'

'Well, Ronnie Withers was wrong, wasn't he? Do you mind if I come in?'

'No, mate, come on through.' He let them in through the front door, and led the way down a dim hall into a back room that abutted a kitchen. Yesterday's *Sun* was on the floor beside the easy chair, and yesterday's pots and pans were still on the draining board in the kitchen. The place was thick with dust and with food smells. 'Haven't had a chance to clean up,' said Mr Coughlan, clearing a place for Charlie by removing the *TV Week* from the other easy chair. 'The missus has been knocked for six by this, I can tell you. Just can't get over it. She'll be in bed still. Don't need her, do you?'

'I expect you can tell me what I need to know,' said Charlie, settling into the chair. 'By the way, your friend Ronnie Withers wasn't entirely wrong.'

'He's sharp, is Ronnie,' said Arthur Coughlan, with an air of acknowledging a pub guru. Charlie leaned forward in his chair to explain what parents always found it difficult to accept.

'Normally there's not much that we can do when teenagers take off, and beyond putting them on a register all we can advise parents to do is wait and hope.'

He had put it as tactfully as possible, but Arthur Coughlan looked even more depressed.

'What's different about Alan, then?' he asked. 'The fact that he's so young?'

Charlie shook his head.

'I'm afraid sixteen isn't all that young, Mr Coughlan. There's kids a lot younger than that sleeping rough in Leeds, and hundreds that age under the bridges in London. No, it's the fact that we had two reported disappearances more or less simultaneously from the same school. That is unusual.'

Arthur Coughlan nodded.

'Is that Katy Bourne? The headmaster asked us about her. His mum and I didn't even know the name, I'm afraid.'

That Charlie had found out already. But the ignorance of parents whose children had left home about even the most mundane aspects of their lives was boundless, in his experience.

'Were there any signs that Alan had a serious new girl-friend in the weeks before he took off?'

'Not that we noticed,' said Arthur Coughlan, positively, for him.

'And you always do get told?'

'It's always clear. He wouldn't sit down and tell us outright. But Alan isn't like some of the kids these days.'

'What exactly do you mean?'

'He has girlfriends. But he isn't the kind who's been sleeping with girls since he was thirteen. That happens, you know. I think it's disgusting. The girls find themselves pregnant before they're anything but children themselves. How can you expect kids to make proper mothers and fathers? Anyway, Alan isn't like that.'

'I didn't say he was, Mr Coughlan. In any case, even if he is having any kind of relationship with this Katy Bourne, it would be unusual for the two of them to go missing together.'

Arthur Coughlan's expression was obstinate.

'I don't think they have gone missing together. Like I say, we never heard the name. We know if Alan has a girlfriend. He'll bring her home, and they'll go up to his room and play records, go to a gig. Then after a few weeks, maybe a couple of months, there'll be a tiff, or they'll both just lose interest. Just like we used to do at his age, Mr Peace.'

Charlie was disconcerted by being classed with a fifty-year-old. Perhaps being a policeman had aged him in people's eyes. He smiled a sort of acceptance, however.

'So for you and your wife, Alan is just a normal teenager?'

'Alan *is* just a normal teenager. And nicer than most.'

'How would you describe him? Describe his character?'

This stumped him.

'He's a nice lad.' Feeling the inadequacy as well as the repetitiousness of this, Mr Coughlan stumbled on. 'He's quite bright at school – expected to do well in his GCSEs. And he's had no particular advantages, because his mother and I have never had much of an education.' He gestured around him. 'It's not a bookish household, as you can see, and that usually makes all the difference, they say. He's never been any trouble – well, you can never say that, can you?

9

Wouldn't be natural. We've had rows, had to lay down the law now and again, but we wouldn't have it any other way, him being a teenager. It's more difficult for them today than it was when I was growing up, with all the nastiness being thrown at them from the television and the newspapers. But Alan's a good lad . . . a good lad.'

He faded into silence. Charlie said gently:

'You'd had a row just before he left home, hadn't you?'

Arthur Coughlan looked at the floor.

'Oh, nothing out of the ordinary. Just about cleaning up his room . . . The normal.'

Charlie's instinct told him this was a lie. He decided to let it be for the moment, till he knew more of the circumstances. He wanted to keep Coughlan on his side.

'Was that on the Friday night?'

'Yes. I don't believe that was why he left home. He was quite normal Saturday breakfast time.'

'But it was Saturday he took off, wasn't it?'

The man nodded, sadly, uncertainly.

'Yes . . . I always go and help out at the Railway Arms Saturday and Sunday lunchtimes. I've been unemployed two years and more, you see, and any little bit of money helps. Used to be a warehouseman at Pickerings, till they went bust.'

'Had your being unemployed caused problems?'

He shook his head emphatically.

'With Alan? Not so you'd notice.' Then he thought for a moment. 'Well, I suppose we did get on each other's nerves in the holidays, but not badly. His mother has a cleaning job with Lloyd's Bank, so she's out early evenings. It's not as though we're all three of us here all the time.'

'Sorry – I interrupted,' said Charlie. 'What happened on Saturday?'

'Well, I went down to the Railway. His mother went to do the weekly shop at Morrisons, then called in at the Railway for her lunch. That's usual. We came back after two, when things quietened down at the pub. Alan wasn't here, but we thought nothing of it. He didn't have to clock in and out.'

10

'When did you start worrying?'

'When he didn't come home for his tea. It was shepherd's pie, his favourite, and he knew that. We rang Darren Sorby, his friend – he hadn't been at theirs. Then we went up to his room.'

He stopped.

'How much had gone?'

'Not everything – not by a long chalk,' said Coughlan firmly. 'That's why I'm sure he means to come home. But all his favourite clothes had gone, quite a few records, some books – including some school books. So I'm sure he intends to go on with school, do his A-levels, like he said he wants.'

Charlie wondered whether he might be clutching at straws. Still, taking books and records did not suggest sleeping rough.

'Doesn't sound as if he thought he'd be on the streets,' he said, encouragingly. 'What did he take all this in?'

'His rucksack. He had a hiking holiday in Northumberland last summer. Was going to take another one this summer.'

'So he didn't take a case?'

'No. Well, he wouldn't. A case to a teenager looks sort of elderly, doesn't it?'

'I suppose so. But somehow it doesn't look as if he expected to stay away for a long time.'

Something in his words aggravated an itching worry in the man's mind.

'Expected . . . A lot of things can happen that you don't expect, if you're sleeping rough.'

'We don't know that he's doing that,' said Charlie, urgently. 'In fact, I'd say it was pretty unlikely. Do you have a recent photograph of him?'

Arthur Coughlan got up and rummaged in a drawer.

'There's his passport photograph,' he said, handing over a European passport. 'It's two years old now. We took him to Spain with us. We didn't care for the place, but he enjoyed it. Oh, and there's this.'

He took a colour snapshot in a cheap frame from the wall unit. It showed a teenager in shorts and short-sleeved shirt, rucksack on his back, smiling into the camera – fresh-faced, a lock of hair straggling over his right eye. Charlie thought it bore out his father's description of him – a nice lad: likeable, responsible.

'Was this on the walking holiday you mentioned?'

'That's right.'

'So quite recent. I'll take this. Does this mean he was on the holiday with a friend?'

'Oh yes. We wouldn't have let him go otherwise. As it was, his mother worried herself sick. He was with Darren Sorby, from his form at school.'

'Perhaps I should talk to Darren. Are they still good friends now?'

'Oh yes. They're mates. Darren's very worried, but we couldn't get anything out of him we didn't know already.'

Charlie took his leave. He had no doubt this man had been a good parent by his lights, but he found both the man and the house dispiriting. He thought he should try to speak to Katy Bourne's parents before he went to the pair's school. She lived a mile and a half away in a little box on an estate of little boxes, built in a hideous orange brick, with a sign at the end of the street saying Pelsett Homes and showing there were still some for sale. These were houses for the newly-married, the newly-divorced, and the old. Katy's box had come out in a rash of lead-lighting. He rang twice and got no answer.

'She won't be back till four,' came a voice. 'She works at the post office in Morley Road.'

There was an elderly couple working in a little scrap of garden next door, and bumping bottoms every time they took a step backwards. It seemed an act of faith to plant anything natural in such an environment. No doubt they had bought the house on retirement, wanting a place where everything was new, and everything would go on working for their lifetime. Fifty per cent right. Charlie strolled over to the knee-high fence.

'Thanks. Is there a Mr Bourne, by the way?'

'No,' said the woman, pushing a strand of hair out of her eyes. 'I'm not sure there ever was. There was a man – I'm pretty sure he wasn't a husband – when they moved in here, but he took off soon afterwards – matter of weeks, so far as I remember.'

'I see. Do you know why?'

'Just said he'd had enough.' She hesitated, then lowered her voice as if the secret police might be listening. 'She's . . . well, not a very sympathetic sort of person.'

'Right. I'll bear that in mind. And the daughter?'

'Oh, very quiet. Don't see much of her. She's not in any trouble, is she?'

'I hope not,' said Charlie, moving off.

The school he drove to, parking with the teachers' cars, was so familiar to him he hardly gave a glance to the peeling paint on the board walls, the ill-fitting windows, the litter-bestrewed playground, and the general air of neglect, as if children would soon be a thing of the past and it wasn't worth spending money on them. The headmaster had been alerted in advance, and was waiting for him.

'I thought you'd want to speak to their best friends,' he said, almost the moment Charlie came into his study, 'so I've alerted them. Darren Sorby and Sharon Reilly.'

'Excellent. But what about you?'

The headmaster, who obviously wanted to shunt him on immediately, spread out his hands.

'We have four hundred pupils here. The most I get is an impression, unless they're problem students or very bright. I've talked to the form teachers though. Alan seems – or seemed, before this – unproblematic: quite good at his work, not a great one for games, hot on the environment. It may not go very deep, but it's a step in the right direction.'

'Sure. And Katy Bourne?'

'Ah, there may be some problems there. Rather a lonely child – adolescent, I should say. It wasn't easy to find a friend of hers. I would say a distinctly unhappy young woman.'

Charlie thought for a moment.

'Unhappy because she's lonely, or lonely because she's unhappy?'

'I think you may be the best person to find that out. You're closer to their age.'

He had made available an unused classroom. There seemed

13

to be plenty of them: school rolls were declining. When the two friends came in Charlie took a desk by the window, through which a fearsome draught beat on his neck, and sat them in two desks on the other side of the aisle.

'Now,' he said, looking first at Darren Sorby, 'I get the sense of Alan Coughlan being fairly bright, well adjusted, with a lot of interests – would that be right?'

Darren Sorby nodded.

'So what went wrong, or what happened? That's not the sort of person who suddenly goes missing as a rule.'

Darren screwed up his mouth.

'Well, he never said anything to me.'

'Had he been any different these last few weeks – or perhaps just the last few days?'

Darren considered this.

'Maybe a bit quieter like. Sort of thoughtful. But you see, we'd just done our GCSEs, so I thought that he was probably worried, or had been overdoing the studying.'

'He was going to stay on at school if he did well?'

'Yes. Or maybe go to the Jakob Kramer College.'

'Did he have any reasons to think that he might have done badly?'

'No. At the time he seemed quite happy with the papers.'

'So how long had he been quiet and thoughtful?'

Darren considered again. He was a slow considerer.

'Difficult to say, really . . . Just a few days, so far as I remember. He was rather quiet on the Wednesday before he took off. We'd been intending to go into town to *The Last Knight*, but then he said he wasn't in the mood.'

'Without giving a reason?'

'No. I'd have said if he had.'

'And you have no reason at all to connect him with Katy Bourne?'

Darren shook his head vigorously.

'No. So far as I know he'd never heard the name. Certainly he'd never mentioned her to me. And he would've if she was his girlfriend, or if he was even interested.'

'She was younger than him, wasn't she?'

14

'Yes, a year younger. But he's had girlfriends in lower years before. It wasn't that.'

Charlie transferred his gaze to Sharon Reilly. The girl was a little overweight, not pretty, but with sharp eyes.

'She never said anything to me. But – '

'But you're not all that close,' supplied Charlie.

'No. And . . . she never told you things. Especially not things like that.'

'Do you mean she was secretive?'

Sharon screwed up her face.

'Not that exactly. More that she was . . . unhappy.' Charlie noted it had been the headmaster's word too, no doubt suggested to him by one of the girl's teachers. 'She didn't think anyone could be interested in her. Didn't think she was *interesting* enough. She could hardly believe it if you made friendly gestures. I think it's what the magazines call low self-esteem.'

Sharon seemed a lot brighter than Darren Sorby. Charlie wondered if it was this that had led to the low-key friendship between her and Katy – wondered whether it was the sort of school where a bright pupil was left very much to herself, and perforce made alliances with other loners.

'I'm guessing the problem was at home,' he suggested quietly. The girl nodded.

'It must have been. She didn't talk about it – not *talk*. But you could tell by her reactions. If her mother was mentioned she went silent, or sometimes made an ugly face. She was sending signals, but she clammed up if you tried to get any details out of her. I tried to help, because I thought it was probably serious, but I never got through to her. There's lots of us don't get on that well with our parents, but this . . .'

'This went deeper?'

'I thought so. That was the impression I got.'

Charlie nodded. He suspected that was the impression the neighbours had had too.

'There was a man, wasn't there, in the household until recently?'

'Yes. Not her father.'

15

'There couldn't be any question of . . . of him and her, him and Katy? . . .'

'Oh, I don't think so. I never got any hint. When he moved out Katy just said he "didn't like the atmosphere – couldn't take it any longer".'

'Well, that tells me something, at least. Did Katy see her natural father?'

'If so, she kept very quiet about it. I never once heard her mention him.'

'Long gone?'

Sharon shrugged.

'For all I know. There's plenty of kids here from one-parent homes. Lots of them don't know who their father is.'

'You think Katy was one of them?'

'That would be my guess. But we weren't that close, you see. Not *friends*.'

'And there was nobody here who was closer?'

'No. I certainly never heard her mention Alan Coughlan, or any other boy as a boyfriend. There was . . . nobody.'

'Bleak.'

The girl considered Charlie's word.

'Yes. I think that's what her life was. Bleak.'

CHAPTER 2

The Mother

There was a light shining behind the lead-lighted windows of Katy Bourne's box. It was a long way from Dingley Dell, but it suggested there was now human habitation. Charlie squared his shoulders for an unsatisfactory encounter and went up and rang the front door bell. Three descending notes and a recorded dog's bark.

Slow footsteps down the hall. The woman who opened the door had a narrow, straight mouth, deep lines of discontent along the forehead, and eyes that were cold and hard. Also tired. No doubt a day spent dispensing pensions, dole money, TV stamps and car licences would take their toll even on a tough lady well capable of taking care of herself.

'Yes?'

'Mrs Bourne?' The woman gave a tentative nod. 'I'm DC Peace,' said Charlie, showing her his ID card and making sure that she read it.

'Oh.'

This time Charlie got a message loud and clear: she was surprised to encounter a black policeman, and not pleased. Or was it that she was not pleased that the police were following up the case at all?

'It's about Katy, Mrs Bourne.'

'Well, I could guess that. Do you want to come in?'

'Please.'

After a second's pause she stood aside and led him into a hallway barely large enough for the two of them, then into a living room that was tiny by any standards, in which paths had been made between the furniture – hand-me-down stuff in a variety of different tastelessnesses. Charlie sat down on a meagrely stuffed chair with wooden arms, conscious of being the first black person to have penetrated this fastness (though he doubted whether visitors of any colour or creed had been frequent occurrences).

'Right. Let's get this over,' was Mrs Bourne's unpromising opener. Charlie took his cue from her and pulled out his notebook.

'Certainly. When did you realize that your daughter had left home, Mrs Bourne?'

'Saturday, when I got home from work. I do one Saturday in four, and that was it.'

'You realized at once she'd gone?'

'Well, no. Just that she wasn't in the house. If she wasn't at school, Katy was usually around the house. I thought she must have forgotten something in the shopping. I had my lunch, and then I began to unpack the shopping she'd left on the kitchen table. That's when I realized.'

'Oh. Why?'

'She'd bought odd amounts. *One* pork chop. Half the milk we usually get. There was more change than there should be. That's when I realized.'

Charlie nodded.

'I suppose you went up to her room?'

'Yes . . . almost everything had gone.'

'How could she have transported all that?' asked Charlie, surprised.

'She didn't have that much. But I did think maybe someone had come and got her.'

'That worried you?'

'It surprised me. I couldn't imagine who it might be.'

Charlie had a sudden insight of these two women, living together in this tiny, unwelcoming box, having only each other and hating each other. Or perhaps – almost as bad – being totally indifferent to each other.

'Did Katy have any contact with her father?' he asked, out of the blue to surprise her. The woman laughed bitterly.

'Don't make me laugh! He took off before she'd even made an appearance.'

'No attempt to make contact since?'

'None. I'd have handed her over soon enough if he'd shown any interest.'

'Did you resent getting pregnant?'

There was a further tightening of the lips.

'I wasn't best pleased.'

'Why did you go through with it?'

Now they were really getting down to basics, to the bed-rock of this woman's hardness and bitterness. There was another laugh – short, shot through with grievance.

'Because he was over the moon. Can you believe what men do to women? He was cock-a-hoop, insisted I had it, said it would be loved. And like a fool I believed him, wanted to hold on to him. So when I was eight months gone, what did he do? He upped and left me. Us, I should say.'

'Leaving you to bring up a baby you had never wanted to have, on your own?'

'That's exactly the size of it. Oh, I had a bit of help from my mother in the early days. But she died of breast cancer five years ago.'

'Did you always resent Katy?'

She shrugged with impatience at the tone or the implications of the question and took out a packet of cigarettes.

'That's the language of books and magazines. I don't need an agony aunt. We just didn't pull together, her and I.'

'Right from the beginning?'

She took a deep draw on her cigarette.

'I didn't get a warm glow from holding her in my arms, if that's what you mean.'

'And your feeling now?'

She tipped her ash angrily into the ashtray and sat four-square. A second or two went by before she replied.

'I was in two minds whether to report her missing, if that answers your question.'

'I think it does. Why did you?'

She shrugged.

'I'd like to know she's all right.'

'You'd rather know she's all right and somewhere else than have her back?'

19

'Frankly, yes.'

'Thank you for being honest with me.' She raised her eye-brows, impervious to or contemptuous of his praise. 'The man who was living here until recently –' Charlie began.

'Harry Tate? Mogadon Man personified. Yes – what about him? He moved out months ago.'

'How did he get on with your daughter?'

'All right.'

The question seemed to astonish her – had obviously never occurred to her. It was as if the man had come to live with her without anybody noticing the fact that he was also coming to live with Katy.

'You don't think there was anything . . . going on between them?'

The laugh this time was heartier.

'There was nothing to speak of "going on" where Harry was concerned. He wasn't much into that sort of thing. In fact he was the original dead loss.'

That verdict seemed to beg a number of questions, includ-ing that of where Harry's tastes lay, and that of whether this woman would have known – or cared – if anything had been going on. Charlie decided to stick with the subject.

'How did you and he get together?'

A wave of annoyance passed over her face. If she was going to be questioned about her own private life, it seemed to say, she regretted that she had ever gone to the police.

'Is that relevant? . . . Oh hell, what's the odds? We met at a pub quiz. When Katy was thirteen I decided she could look after herself and I could get out and about more. I found I was good at pub quizzes – won prizes, which came in useful. I always had a good memory. We teamed up, and when he suggested he move in with us, I thought his money would come in useful to pay the mortgage on this place.'

'But it didn't work out?'

'The money was useful, but he was useless.'

'Did you throw him out, or did he leave?'

'Let's just call it mutual consent. I found I could manage the mortgage, with difficulty, and he'd helped with the move, and I thought he'd served his turn. We didn't need his pity.'

Charlie pricked up his ears, and she noticed and immediately showed she regretted letting something out.

'His pity?'

She stubbed out her cigarette abruptly.

'He was sorry for Katy. He said she was lonely and unloved. So what? I'm lonely and unloved, aren't I? It was better we sort it out on our own.'

'I suppose you could say in a way it has sorted itself, at least for the moment,' said Charlie. She looked at him stonily. 'You've said already you won't mind being on your own, if that's how things turn out.'

'I won't. At least it simplifies things. And I can suit myself, without any critical eyes on me.'

Charlie left a moment's pause.

'This boy, Alan Coughlan – had you ever heard your daughter mention him?'

'No, I hadn't. Have you talked to his parents?'

'To his father, yes.'

'Well, if there was anything going on, they'd know. When he rang, his father said the boy always brought his girlfriends home. They knew nothing about Katy, so I should think there's nothing in the idea.'

'You apparently don't think Katy would have told you.'

'I'm damned sure she wouldn't.'

She seemed to take an obscure pride in that.

'And if you had to hazard a guess as to whether she had a boyfriend at the moment – ?'

'If I had to hazard a guess on the probable course of Katy's love life, I'd say she was unlikely to have a boyfriend till she was in her twenties – middle or late twenties at that – and that when it happened they'd both be pretty desperate, and the chances of him being Mr Right were practically nil. Mind you, the chances of finding Mr Right are practically nil anyway, so why should Katy have more luck than anybody else? Other people will just have more fun testing out possibilities, that's all.'

'You find life pretty unsatisfactory, don't you?'

'Totally. That's why I'm better on my own.'

Charlie thought that was probably a hint.

'So, summing up, there's no one you could imagine Katy having gone to – friend, relative or whatever?'

'None. If I could think of anybody I'd have rung them up. I'm not totally uninterested. I'm just not particularly concerned. Don't think I'm alone in that. A great many parents feel exactly the same.'

'Oh, I know, I know. That's why a lot of kids go missing, and that's why a lot of them stay missing without anybody caring very much one way or the other.' He paused, thinking. 'But I must say this doesn't feel very much like an adolescent just leaving home to live on the streets.'

'I hope you're right. Now, if you've finished, I've had a hard day and I've got a meal to cook –'

They stood up, both feeling slightly awkward.

'Mrs Bourne –'

'Miss. I've never been married.'

'– if we find out where Katy is, what should we do? If she's not in any danger, there's little point in bringing her back here, particularly when the likelihood is she's just going to take off again. On the other hand, she's only fifteen.'

'You've answered your own question. There's no point in dragging her back if she'll leave home again the minute I go to work. Fifteen is grown up these days anyway.'

'Not in the eyes of the law it isn't,' said Charlie firmly. 'And there's the question of school.'

'We can face up to that come the autumn,' said her mother dismissively. 'Anyway, the number of kids round here who spend their time skiving off school – when they're not actually excluded – doesn't suggest it will be a problem.'

It was true enough. Even compared with his younger days school seemed to have become an option rather than a legal requirement. Yet it stuck in the throat that this woman gave the impression of having rehearsed in advance the arguments for not acting and not caring. Anything he said had to sound feeble.

'We'll keep in touch,' he said at the door.

'Suit yourself,' she replied, shutting it.

*   *   *

As it turned out, Charlie had to ring Katy's mother a couple of days later. He had had a visit at police headquarters from Arthur Coughlan, and when he had been summoned down to the outer office the man's face showed something close to animation.

'I wanted to tell you it's all right – about Alan, I mean.'

'Oh? He's come home?'

'Well, no . . . Not yet he hasn't. But we've had a phone call from him, and he's all right.'

Charlie nodded, not too discouragingly.

'That's good news. He didn't say where he was?'

'No. But he was calling from a house, not a phone box. I could hear voices in the background, and a television or a radio on.'

'You didn't think of calling 1471 and getting the number he'd been ringing from?'

The man looked blank.

'I didn't know you could do that.'

'Never mind. Not a lot do. Did he say why he'd left home, or when he'd be back?'

The man looked awkward.

'Not really. But he said he would be back . . . And he said that Katy Bourne was there too.'

That did surprise Charlie.

'I see. Did you ask him whether he and she were . . . involved with each other?'

'Sort of. Didn't quite know how to put it, but he got my point eventually. He said no. Well, what he actually said was: "You just don't understand, Dad. You never do." You know how teenagers feel. They never think you've been a teenager yourself.'

It was an understandable feeling, Charlie thought, as far as Arthur Coughlan was concerned.

'But you definitely got the impression that, though they're both at the same place, they're not together in any other sense?'

'Definitely.'

'Odd.'

'I don't see why,' said Coughlan, with a weak man's obstinacy. 'It's cheered his mother up no end, I can tell you. He's obviously all right, with a roof over his head.'

Charlie had to bite back the retort that it was possible to be very far from all right, even with a roof over one's head. This was hardly a police matter any more, so far as he could tell.

'Well, it's all encouraging,' he said. 'I'll ring up Katy's mother later.'

'Oh, we've done that – did it straight away. To tell you the truth, she didn't sound very interested.'

She sounded even less interested when, for form's sake, Charlie rang her that same evening.

'Oh yes, that Coughlan man rang me up. It seems they've got a place of some kind or other. Sounds like a satisfactory solution to me.'

'Certainly I don't think the police need to be involved any longer,' said Charlie. His implication that a mother might want to be fell on predictably stony ground.

'Oh no. Forget about the whole thing. Let them get on with it.'

And that, for the time being, was what everyone did.

CHAPTER 3

The Centre

'That lazy cow Bett Southcott won't come and do the potatoes,' said Katy Bourne, coming into the kitchen of 24 Portland Terrace. 'Says she's not feeling well. If I had my way she wouldn't get any supper.'

'That's not Ben's way,' said Alan, reaching down into a low cupboard for a large saucepan.

'Not Ben's way at all,' agreed Katy. '"These are seriously disturbed youngsters." Oh well, just so long as he sticks to his promise that if they don't pull their weight over the long term they won't be allowed back.'

She pulled a bag of potatoes from the vegetable rack, and set to with a peeler. Alan watched her with affection. She was coming along, was Katy. Three weeks before, when they had both come to number twenty-four, she would hardly have ventured an opinion of her own – not an unfavourable view of one of the people at the Centre, and certainly not an implied criticism of Ben. And she wouldn't have used the word 'cow' either. She was getting opinions, getting a character.

Or rather the character that had always been there, submerged and suppressed, was beginning to emerge, to shake itself after slumber and walk tall. That was how Alan saw her, anyway. If challenged he would have had to admit that at school he had barely noticed her. Now, putting together the odd thing she had told him about her home life, so very different and so much sadder than his own, he saw that any life she had had must have taken place below a surface where practically nothing of any moment was discernible.

'How many tonight?' he asked conversationally. Katy was peeling the potatoes with the skill of a school dinner lady.

'Eight,' she said, not stopping. 'Kelly Smith left today, and nobody's come.'

'I wouldn't bank on that. Evening's the time they come, and it was quite chilly out.'

Ten minutes later he was proved right. There was a ring on the front door bell, and since Ben was out he went to answer it himself. That was something Katy still didn't like doing, though she would do it if necessary.

'Thought so,' he said when he came back. 'There'll be nine.'

'Anyone we know?' Katy asked.

'No, new. Lad of my age, or younger . . . Some of them are so *young*.'

'I know.'

There was silence for a few moments. The implications of that were difficult to cope with, especially for Katy. She was happier now than she had ever been, but she didn't know how she would manage alone on the streets.

'Where did you put him?'

'In the empty half of the front room of twenty-two, next to Zak. He'll be all right with Zak.'

'Everyone's all right with Zak. Zak's gentle.'

Alan nodded. Zak was gentle, safe. Not all of them were.

'Zak's out the day after tomorrow,' Alan said. 'But he can show the new boy the ropes before then.'

'Such as they are. Are you going to start the stew?'

'Yes. Everything's ready.' He turned on the large electric frying pan. 'You know, they *ought* to come and help with the cooking when it's their turn.'

'Of course they should. This isn't a hotel.'

'Cooking's a skill,' said Alan, in his serious, thoughtful way, 'a survival skill. It's just what they need, and it's not difficult to learn. Just think – three weeks ago I couldn't have cooked a stew to save my life. Now . . . even if it is a bit basic, it's perfectly good food.'

'Basic is what it should be. The more frills there are, the sooner Ben's money will run out.'

It was true they rang the changes on a fairly small repertory when preparing supper. For a start, they tried to cook meals that the young people could take to their rooms and eat off their lap if that's what they preferred. Some of them were not into socializing, as they put it. So there were stews, meatballs, lasagne, shepherd's pie, casseroles. A lot of mince was consumed. Alan was confident in about three of the variations, and preferred it when it was mince. Cutting up meat for eight plus the three of them had been hard work, and it had taken time. Katy was a lot better, and could manage all of the dishes. She even had plans for some new ones. She'd done a lot of cooking for herself in her time. Alan always watched her when she was cooking something he couldn't manage, and then decided which one he would try his hand at next.

The smell of onion began to fill the kitchen. It had always been one of Alan's favourite smells.

'The sad thing is, most of them would prefer hamburgers anyway,' said Katy.

'To quote Ben: "Junk food is what they get when they're on the streets, not what we give them when they're here."'

'He's right, of course.' They looked at each other and grinned. 'He generally is.'

So that day they prepared the meal without any help and listened to the comings and goings in the house and from the house next door. Many of the temporary residents begged in the centre of Leeds, or busked, and Ben had set the mealtime for seven thirty to enable them to get what they could out of the commuters going for their evening trains and buses, and then get themselves home. Many of them preferred to walk, as they were not welcome on public transport. They were allowed a fortnight's residence, then had to go, and they could not get back unless they had been gone for at least a fortnight. They could use the address for purposes of receiving mail, however – important in the matter of receiving benefits, those few of them who did, and now and again of resuming contact with their families. This did not often happen though. Sometimes, heartbreakingly, the young people themselves tried to make contact, but got no response.

Ben had said he would be busy all afternoon, and didn't know when in the evening he would be back. At twenty past seven Alan took the frying pan through to the big front room of number twenty-four, and Katy followed with a big saucepan full of mashed potatoes, and then fetched the plate with a large pile of bread. To get the maximum number sitting down to a meal there were two small tables, one by the window, the other by the door. Five could be squeezed on to each of them, but it was usually unnecessary: if no one wanted to eat in their room, most of them were perfectly happy to sit around the wall and fork in the food. Many of them were unused to proper mealtimes: once when they had had pork chops (because they were on offer) several had had to be taught how to cut them up. At least, Alan thought, we sat round to a proper meal on Sundays at home.

Zak was the first through from number twenty-two, with his dog Pal and the new arrival, who looked around him very unsure of himself but got a sparkle in his eye when he saw the food on the table. He clearly hadn't eaten for some time. Pal settled down with a sigh close to the table by the window. Dogs were allowed, but only one in each house unless they were dogs who were already well acquainted from life on the streets. Pal was Zak's best friend, and nobody doubted Zak when he said that he went hungry before he let Pal want for food. Pal was a lean, two-toned mongrel, but his leanness was in his metabolism, and it was worth its weight, or lack of it, when Zak sat in Albion Street with his capacious beret in front of them. Zak wasn't his real name. Nobody knew what his real name was, and nobody asked.

Rose came in next. Rose came from what was conventionally called a 'good' family – one which was bad in every human sense of the word. Katy identified with Rose, and tried to get close to her, but that was nearly impossible. Rose said almost nothing, drifted along inside or outside the Centre as if in a dream, and generally gave the impression that her mind was busy constructing a novel system of metaphysics.

Gradually they all wandered in. Alan served the stew, Katy

the mash, and everyone helped themselves to bread and marge. Alan and Katy made sure they gave a bit extra to those who would be going back on the streets in the next day or two. They needed fattening up, though less now that the nights were warmer than they would in the viciously cold winter months.

Katy served the last of them, and then took the empty chair next to Tony. Tony was younger than her, only fourteen. He was not even old for his age, certainly not vicious. He was chattering away now about the events of his day, begging in Leeds, how he'd dodged the occasional policeman on his beat, about the 'silly old git' who told him he should be in school. Katy had never heard from him the reasons he was on the streets. Others, particularly the girls, had horrendous home backgrounds, histories of sexual or physical abuse, but she had never heard any such thing from Tony, or had any impression of terrors in his past. But he was something special to her, and if she had been able to analyse her emotions with the sophistication of an adult she would have seen her concern for him as maternal. On his other side sat Splat, with the rings in his nose and ears, his tattooed neck and hands, his red-and-blue-dyed hair. Splat only came occasionally for a day or two. His natural home was the streets. There was nothing particular wrong with Splat, but when the thought occurred to Katy that he was Tony's future, she shivered.

They were all of them getting to the end of their main course when Ben came home. He pushed open the dining-room door, greeted them all cheerfully, then quietly took a plate and helped himself to stew and mashed potatoes.

'There's a bit left,' he said. 'Anybody want it, or shall we give it to Pal?'

'Pal's done all right,' said Zak, tweaking his ears. 'With twelve to beg from he always does.'

The stew was claimed, a spoonful each, by Tony, by the new arrival, and by Bett Southcott, a tall, thin girl with a discontented expression, who always seemed to be hungry. Ben took his plate and sat down against the wall, quite relaxed, forking the food in. Alan suspected that basic food suited Ben because he had never been very interested in what he ate. Ben's great quality was stillness. Alan could imagine the Centre being run – and run well – by a genial sergeant-major type, for example, with a rod of iron. But Ben was quiet and reserved, listened when people wanted to talk, tried to be always there but only to be noticed when he was needed or could be of help. Alan wondered, not for the first time, what he had done with the first forty-odd years of his life.

The meal ended with fresh fruit. 'Why stew it when it's much nicer fresh?' Ben always said. It was Zak's turn to wash up, and he and Pal went off quite happily with piles of plates and cutlery to the kitchen. The others dispersed: a couple to a pub where they could drink outside without arousing hostility, most to their rooms.

'That lazy cow Bett Southcott ought to help Zak,' said Katy to Ben. 'She refused to do the potatoes, but she came down soon enough to eat her share and anything else going.'

'She's resentful about something,' said Ben equably. 'I expect she'll talk about it one of these days. Could I have a word with you two, alone?'

They went round to number twenty-two and upstairs to Ben's bedroom – the only room in the two houses that had not been redecorated, and the only room that was really his in the two adjacent houses that he owned. It was like a monk's cell with a few modern additions. It had a bed, a desk, a couple of chairs and a collection of books and LPs – Ben hadn't caught up with the CD revolution. Katy thought there ought to be photographs, and wondered why there weren't. Ben lay on the bed, and Katy and Alan took chairs. They liked it when Ben talked things through with them.

'I went to see Dickie Mavors today,' he began, talking quietly and unhurriedly. 'He's the Leeds City Council member for the Bramsey district.'

'Why did you go?'

Ben paused.

'Someone rang from the Bramsey Tory Party headquarters. Said there was beginning to be talk.'

They took some time to digest this.

'What's he like, this Mavors?' asked Katy.

'Amiable enough old body. Bit of a dodderer. Getting past his sell-by date electorally, and is beginning to realize it. Still, responding to local pressures has been his life. He's been where he is for the past twenty years or more, and probably politically active before that. I don't think we can look to him to take a stand on our behalf.'

'Why should we need someone to do that?' Alan demanded with adolescent belligerence.

'I don't think we do – yet. But he naturally asked questions. Safety. Did they pay for their bed or their food? What kind of young people did we take in? Drugs, of course.'

'Well, he can't get us there. That's one thing you've always been firm on,' said Alan.

'Yes,' said Ben, reflectively. 'For one good and simple reason: we're not capable of facing the problems that drugs involve. I have no experience of it, and the good advice of a well-meaning amateur is worse than useless. If they have a drugs problem they don't come here. Frankly, that rules out a large proportion of the young homeless in Leeds. Sad, not at all what I'd like, but inevitable at the moment.'

'But it means the ones who do come here are fairly new to the streets,' Katy pointed out.

'Yes. Not all, but a good number.'

'I just don't see how anyone could object to what you're doing!' she protested passionately.

'Oh, property values, undesirable influence on the local kids – there are any number of reasons you can think up when what you mean is you want your little spot to remain as it always has been, and that whatever needs to be done about the problem people of this world, it shouldn't be done in your back yard.'

'But where does all this leave us?' Alan demanded.

'I don't know . . .' Ben remained silent for a bit, his deep blue eyes focused on a distant prospect that was not the peeling wall of his bedsitting room. 'Maybe register the place as a hostel,' he said at last. 'Maybe form a charitable trust, have more rules and regulations.'

'But being unofficial and having no rules to speak of is

what makes them feel safe in coming to us!' protested Katy.

'I know. I'm certainly not going to try to get us accepted into the System if I can avoid it. But rules and regulations can be unofficial, known only to us . . .'

'That sounds underhand,' said Katy, and Alan nodded. 'What kind of rules and regulations are you thinking of?'

'Maybe we have to be careful about the underage dossers we take in,' Ben said, reluctantly.

'But it is people like Tony who are just the ones who need us most!' Katy said, and again Alan nodded.

'Yes,' agreed Ben. 'Or so we like to think. Maybe I should talk to them more, find out where they come from, what their background is. For example, I never heard of any reason why Tony couldn't go back home. What if we are just prolonging things for them by making a life on the streets more bearable? I certainly wouldn't encourage them to go back to be abused all over again, but obviously if they've got a good home and their parents are sick with worry that's another matter . . . And you two should ring your parents regularly.'

Katy pushed out her lower lip.

'It *looks* better, if anything comes up,' insisted Ben. 'If what you say is true, your mother won't do anything about it.'

'We'll do it,' said Alan firmly, looking at Katy. She nodded. 'Meanwhile?'

'Meanwhile, I suppose we go on as before,' said Ben, stroking his chin. 'But we'll be more careful – who we take in, for example. And we'll be especially nice to neighbours. If we're beginning to be a "problem", it's the neighbours who are making us one.'

When Katy rang her mother later that evening, she was very conscious of the thumping of her heart.

'Hello, Mum.'

There was a second or two's pause at the other end of the line.

'Well, this is unexpected.'

'I just thought I'd let you know I'm all right.'

'Yes – I had the message from that Coughlan man . . . Am I allowed to ask what you're doing?'

'I'm doing something useful.'

'Well, *that* could cover a multitude of sins!'

'Oh, *Mum*! I'm helping people.'

'That could be taken several ways, too . . . Oh, all right: forget I said anything. Well, your room's still here – I haven't let it or anything.'

That was a concession, and Katy recognized it as such.

'That's good, Mum. I'll be back to see you when we're less busy . . .'Bye for now.'

Katy's mother had often said 'I'm all right on my own', usually looking hard at Katy when she said it. After the phone call Katy wondered if she was finding it quite as pleasant as she had expected, being on her own.

Alan's phone call to his parents was altogether more relaxed.

'Hello, Mum. Glad you're up and about again.'

'Alan! Well, now I know you're all right . . . You are all right, aren't you, Alan?'

'Never better, Mum. Busy, but I like that.'

'But what are you *doing*, Alan?'

'Something useful, Mum. Working real hard.'

'But why, Alan? This is your holiday. School's broken up now. You've just done your GCSEs, and you deserve a break.'

'A break is what I'm getting, Mum – a clean break . . . I felt knocked for six, Mum – by you know what. I feel better if I keep busy. Don't *worry*, Mum. And tell Dad not to as well. I'll keep in touch. 'Bye, Mum.'

His mother and father had discussed what to do if he rang again, and the moment she had put the phone down she took it up again and rang the call return facility on 1471 to find out the number he had rung home from.

CHAPTER 4

Face to Face

When she had been told the number Alan had rung her from, Mrs Coughlan got straight on to Charlie Peace at police headquarters. Her mind was now comparatively at rest: she thought she knew that Alan was safe and well, but she did very much want to know *where* he was, and what he was doing. She was in many ways an old-fashioned mother: the idea that Alan had some rights to privacy and independence at sixteen would have seemed to her quite silly. When she had given Charlie the number he said he'd get back to her, then went straight down to Records to see what he could find out about the person and place behind the number.

'It's a domestic property, 24 Portland Terrace,' said the sergeant in charge, a young, enthusiastic snapper-up of unconsidered trifles. 'We had some complaints back in April, when it had recently changed hands. Now owned by a Benjamin Marchant. The complaints, by the way, seemed to be orchestrated – two neighbours ringing on successive days and talking about drugs. We sent a man round, but there didn't seem to be anything in it. Lots of young people, but no signs of drugs on the premises.'

'Young people?' queried Charlie. 'Do you mean he's running some kind of lodging house for DSS cases?'

The Records sergeant shook his head.

'No, that didn't seem to be it. No money changed hands. The man who went round said that this Marchant was setting up some kind of unofficial refuge for young homeless people.'

'Unofficial? So no connection with Shelter, the Sally Army, or people like that?'

'No. Completely unofficial. They just call it the Centre, and rely on word of mouth to get it known. It was just beginning then, but the PC said that Marchant was aiming to provide short-term stays for young people on the streets.'

'I must say I wasn't expecting my two to be on the streets. If they have been, they've found a roof over their heads pretty sharpish. Any more complaints?'

'Another ten days ago, but very vague. "Terrible-looking young people with dyed hair and rings in their noses" – that kind of thing. We didn't follow it up.'

'Anything on this Benjamin Marchant?'

'Nothing you could call a record. Maintenance order served on somebody of that name in 1982 . . . Done a flit. Could be a different bloke. That's it.'

'Not very much. I don't feel I'm really getting the picture. Anyway, I'll have to go and talk to my two. I think the boy might be persuaded to go home. I'm not sure about the girl, and she's the younger, and in more danger. Assuming they're together, the boy could probably be more useful as protection for her if he stays put.'

It was late morning before Charlie could get away from routine paperwork at police HQ. When he got to Bramsey he left the police car around the corner, well away from 24 Portland Terrace. He didn't want to frighten the people in the refuge, or give the neighbours who were agitated the wrong idea. He was very conscious of the fact that a few years ago he might have been taken for one of the homeless refuge-seekers, whereas now he looked almost frighteningly respectable. It occurred to him that his very smartness might reduce his usefulness as a black police detective. He took off his jacket, loosened his tie and lingered on the corner, looking down Portland Terrace.

The street seemed mostly to have been built around the turn of the century: tall, narrow houses, with the attics converted into third-storey bedrooms. Mostly they were terraced, and a lane at the back gave access to a yard and kitchen door. Here and there, in gaps, later, smaller houses had been inserted, their walls abutting their neighbours', looking like children holding the hands of grown-ups on either side. Most of the houses looked solid but neglected – stalwart presences gone to seed with age. It was not unlike Alan's home street.

As he watched, two young people rounded the far corner from him, carrying bulging supermarket bags in both their hands. He lingered, noticing the house numbers nearest to him, and doing a quick calculation in his head. As they came nearer he thought he recognized Alan Coughlan from the last year's photograph he had been given by the boy's father. The pair, talking animatedly, turned into number twenty-four. They didn't look like any homeless adolescents he had ever seen. It looked as if they were doing good rather than taking refuge. He lingered, to give them time to disburden themselves of their loads. Then he walked down the Terrace and rang the doorbell.

'Alan Coughlan?' he said to the boy in the short-sleeved shirt and baggy trousers who opened the door with an expression that was almost welcoming. 'I'm D C Peace.'

The boy took some time to register the abbreviation, then his expression lost its welcome. He barely looked at the ID put in front of his eyes, and stood four-square in the doorway as if to repel the invader.

'Yes?'

'Can I come in and talk to you?'

'Why?'

Charlie had to tell himself he had been twice as bolshie as this at his age, especially with policemen.

'Because you're sixteen years old and missing from home,' he said reasonably, 'and Katy Bourne is fifteen years old and missing from home. All right?'

The boy hesitated, then reluctantly stood aside. Charlie walked down the long, high hallway, noting the new paint and the attempt at cheerfulness in the colours. A side door led into a large sitting room, which in its turn opened directly into a kitchen. In there Katy Bourne was stuffing food from the supermarket into over-full cupboards, items now and then falling out on to the table tops and cooker.

'There's no beds tonight, Alan –' she began, and then turned around. 'Oh.'

Clearly his relaxation of his smartness had not turned Charlie into a likely dosser.

'Katy Bourne?' he asked. She nodded slowly. 'Do you think you could come through into this room, and we can all have a talk? I'm DC Peace, by the way.'

'DC?'

'Detective Constable. I'm a policeman.'

She came through, but dragging her feet. The set of her shoulders reminded him of her mother: she was going to be awkward.

'There is nothing illegal going on here, you know – no drugs or anything, no prostitution. This isn't that kind of place. It's a sort of hostel – a refuge.'

'It's you I'm here about, not the refuge. Now, can we all sit down?'

He set an example by sinking into an armchair. They slowly sat down on the sofa, close but not intimately close. He looked them over as he took out his notebook. Alan Coughlan was nice-looking without being in any way handsome or distinguished – Charlie had known boys of his age look distinguished, against all the odds. A lock of hair fell over his right eye, and his face was lean, with sharp eyes twinkling from under fair eyelashes. It was the eyes that gave Charlie the idea that he was going to grow up an interesting man – not an insurance tout or a bank manager anyway (Charlie had had a bad experience recently with the manager of a bank which claimed to fall over backwards in its eagerness to hand out loans).

Katy was of course more unformed, further back on the road to womanhood. Her clothes seemed to have been bought with little idea about colour or fit – just something to drape over herself. Charlie wondered whether this was her doing or her mother's. But in her case, too, the face was alive, with bright eyes and mobile mouth, and this was not something he had expected from her friend's or her mother's account of her. He could only assume that it was since she had left home that she had come alive. Certainly her whole stance on the sofa suggested an attitude that was positive and even, if necessary, aggressive.

'Now –' began Charlie.

'I don't see why you're here,' said Katy, who clearly believed in the pre-emptive strike. 'We've rung our parents; they know we're all right.'

'They know you say you're all right,' corrected Charlie. 'On the other hand, you were careful not to tell them where you were or what you are doing.'

'I suppose mine used the call return facility, did they?' asked Alan. 'I must say I would never have thought they'd heard of it.'

Charlie refrained from mentioning that he'd had to tell them about it.

'Naturally they're concerned about you,' he began. Katy Bourne shook her head vigorously.

'You're just saying that,' she protested. 'It's just words. My mother isn't concerned in the least.'

'Of course she is.'

'She isn't finding life alone as pleasant as she had hoped, and she isn't liking having to do the things I used to do, but that's *all*. She isn't concerned about me at all. The person she's concerned about is herself.'

Charlie thought he'd better try a new tack.

'How did you come to leave home?' he asked.

'We heard about this place, and we thought we could do useful work here,' said Alan, 'at least over the summer, and maybe for longer.'

'You'd had a row at home, hadn't you?' Charlie probed. 'What was it about?'

'Oh – the usual things,' Alan said, with studied vagueness and shrugging his shoulders. 'Being out late, playing loud music, that kind of thing.'

It was the first time during the interview he had lied. It was done with a sort of schoolboy aplomb, but was none the more convincing for that.

'So you'd both heard of this place . . . Who from?'

'Oh, several people. There's a number of people of my age at school who've left home for a bit.'

The vagueness clearly masked another lie.

'And you, Katy?'

'Oh . . . the same.'

Charlie shifted in his chair. Was it worth trying to batter down this particular wall?

'What attracted you to homeless young people as the sort of area you wanted to work in?'

'Isn't it obvious?' said Katy, with renewed fierceness. 'These are people of our own age, sometimes younger. They've got no homes, often no family that wants to have anything to do with them. They can't get benefits, they can't get a job. So, they've just fallen through the system. They beg, they do drugs, they fall into prostitution. Of course we're concerned. They could be me.'

That speech, at least, had the ring of truth. Charlie turned to Alan.

'But it couldn't be you, could it, Alan?'

'Of course it could.'

'You've got parents who are concerned about you, a good, stable home, you are doing well at school.'

Alan seemed on the edge of saying something revealing, but then he changed his mind.

'Being homeless can happen to anyone,' he said. It was true enough for Charlie to change his tack.

'OK, tell me about this hostel.'

'I knew you were wanting to get dirt on the Centre,' said Katy.

'Only because you two are here,' said Charlie equably. 'Who comes here, who runs it?'

'The young homeless on the streets in Leeds come here,' said Alan. 'They can stay a fortnight, then they have to leave for a bit. We don't take anyone who's into drugs, since that's a special problem we can't deal with because you need special skills. Anyone who's going to be disruptive for the rest isn't allowed back in. Otherwise, we take everyone we can, and there are practically no rules.'

It occurred to Charlie that there were points in this account where it would have been natural to use the name of the man running the refuge, but Alan had avoided it.

'Who started it, who runs it?' Charlie asked. Alan paused, and pursed his lips, but concluded it would be foolishly suspicious to keep the name back.

'Ben. Ben Marchant. He started it and runs it.'

'How long's it been going?'

'Three months or so.'

'And what does he run it on?'

'They don't pay,' said Katy quickly. She'd been told that would make a difference legally, Charlie felt sure. 'They live here free and get a meal a day.'

'So what does Ben do for money?'

'He got a lottery win,' said Alan. 'Not millions and millions, but a nice sum. He bought the two houses with it, did them up, then started up the Centre.'

'Why?'

'Because he wanted to help, put something back. He's a good bloke. He wants to do good.'

'Can I talk to him?'

'No, he's out. But I'm sure he'd talk to you if he were here. We've got nothing to hide.'

'I didn't say you had . . . Will you go back home when the school holidays end?'

They both looked down.

'I may,' said Alan. 'I want to keep on with school.'

Katy looked up, an obstinate expression on her face.

'I don't want to go back, ever,' she said.

'You're too young to have left home, you know,' Charlie said gently.

Katy's chin went up.

'I'm not. There's younger than me here.'

'I don't doubt it. We do have experience in the police, you know, of the people who are on the streets. That doesn't alter the fact that you're both too young. The danger is, you'll get into a downward spiral – you'll have seen that here. Will you go back and see your parents? It would help. Help us to turn a blind eye to the situation, for the moment.'

That was a new thought. Some of the hostility went out of the set of their shoulders. After a moment they both nodded.

'Well,' said Charlie, getting up. 'I'm not sure there's much else I can do at the moment. There doesn't seem to be anything to be gained by hauling you both back to your parents, only to have you take off again. But' – he turned to Alan – 'you are the older, and I hold you responsible for Katy's welfare. If there is anything going on here that makes you uneasy, you get in touch with me – right?'

This time there was no hesitation in the boy's nodded response. When they said goodbye they were both almost friendly.

As he walked back to the car Charlie mulled over his impressions of Alan Coughlan. From the little he had learnt from his father he had got the picture of a normal boyhood in the nineties: fairly good at schoolwork, fashionable interests of the young, worry about future employment prospects – generally happy, or at least contented, and socially concerned.

And then, suddenly, something different. There was something *more* about the Alan Coughlan he had just seen. There was a stretching out towards maturity – and he had the feeling that it was due to something that had happened. It embraced in embryo all the aspects that maturity does embrace – considered responses, acceptance of responsibility, and ability to rise above his own egotistical concerns. If only the boy had not held back at that moment when he seemed to be about to say something revelatory. Or perhaps, knowing young people, what he had been about to say might have seemed revelatory to the boy himself, but would have seemed utterly trivial or beside the point to an outsider. Still, Charlie itched to know what had made the boy take that giant leap towards adulthood.

He got into his car and directed it towards the Coughlan family home.

He was pleased when the door was opened by Alan's mother. It was his first sight of her. She was fair, plump, mid-forties or later – a comfortable, undemanding mother, and obviously a loving one, though perhaps not a strong one in a crisis. She presented a pleasant contrast and comparison to Katy's self-absorbed parent.

'Oh – you must be Mr Peace. Come in. Have you got any news?'

Charlie went through to the living room – tidier now, indeed well scrubbed and polished. Knowing her son was all right had clearly brought out Mrs Coughlan's house-proud instincts.

'Yes, I have,' he said, sitting down. 'I've just come from talking to him and Katy Bourne. I don't think they're together – I mean not romantically involved in any way. They're working – and working very hard, I would guess – at a sort of hostel or refuge for homeless young people in Bramsey.'

Her face fell a little.

'Oh dear. I don't like the sound of that. I couldn't bear it if Alan got into drugs and that. There's someone at the bank that happened to, and she felt she just lost her daughter – she said it was like another person being in the same body.'

Charlie held up his hand.

'Don't jump the gun, Mrs Coughlan! We did investigate the place a while ago and there was no evidence of drugs. As far as we could see – and as far as I could judge today – the place provides a bit of stability for young people who've dropped out. I would think that Alan is doing a very useful job there.'

'Yes, but –'

'He's so young. I know. But some time before very long you were going to lose him, he was going to fly the nest.'

'But *sixteen*!'

'I know. Children grow up younger than in your day, Mrs Coughlan. They have to. They're getting adult messages thrown at them all the time from school, from the media – even from the pop songs. What do you think made him leave home?'

'Well, we had this row . . . about tidying his room.'

Charlie had to stop himself raising his eyebrows.

'And yet he seems to have been a happy, normal boy before.'

'Oh, he *was*.' She seized on his words as if they were a self-justification. 'Always happy, always helpful. Alan was

42

never a rebel. And Arthur has always been good to him. We tried to be sensible – made his girlfriends welcome, let him go on holidays with a friend, did everything we could for him money-wise, though that hasn't been easy these last few years, what with Arthur on the dole, and only the odd bit of extra money coming in. He's down the Railway at the moment, helping. They're doing a wedding.'

Something in her words struck Charlie, and as she chattered on he tried to work out what it was. He interrupted her.

'Mrs Coughlan, is your husband Alan's natural father?'

It had been the words 'Arthur has always been good to him'. As if he had somehow taken Alan on. Mrs Coughlan looked down into her lap.

'No, he isn't. I married him when Alan was one.'

'And did Alan find out about this? Was that what the row was really about?'

It was a moment before she replied.

'Yes. Yes, it was.'

'Would you tell me the name of Alan's real father?'

She looked up, visibly distressed.

'Oh, surely we don't have to rake all that up again, do we? I know I'm old-fashioned, and it's a bit ridiculous in the circumstances, but I don't like talking about it – it embarrasses me, and –'

'Was his name Ben Marchant?'

There was silence, and then she nodded.

'Yes. Ben was Alan's father. I haven't seen him for years.'

And Charlie was willing to bet that Ben was also the man who Mrs Bourne hadn't seen since shortly before the birth of Katy.

CHAPTER 5

Outside Interest

Mrs Alicia Ingram was quiet during dinner. She had cooked for her husband the sort of varied and delicate meal she cooked when she had little dinner parties for people who mattered, or might matter, though perhaps with less care and attention, for Alicia Ingram was someone with a strict sense of priorities. But she had eaten it with an absorbed air, staring at the cloth, her fine red hair flowing down her shoulders in more abandon than usual, her ample (but not too) bosom held back from the strawberry granita, her little red mouth pursed.

Her husband knew exactly what she was going to say, and eventually she said it.

'I'm going to go for the candidacy, Randolph.'

His mouth did not show the tiny smile of self-congratulation that he was feeling.

'Are you, Alicia?' he said, feigning mild surprise. 'I'd have thought you'd be wiser to wait for Dickie Mavors to announce his intention of retiring?'

'Oh –' she brushed this aside with a reddened spoon. 'He should have gone years ago. The Bramsey ward needs some-one with twenty times his energy.'

'Well, it's your business not mine,' said Randolph, who was not even a member of the party, 'but I'd have thought you'd best go carefully. There's plenty around who would like to take Dickie Mavors's place on Leeds City Council.'

He had done his duty – warned his wife. She was, he knew, not wonderfully well-liked in Bramsey Conservative circles. Her manner was a bit domineering, and though it was a gross exaggeration to say, as some did, that she oozed condescension as Liz Taylor oozed diamonds, still the tone of voice in which she spoke to people, the way she looked at them, grated on many. The trouble was, she had a need not only to feel superior to people, but to show them just how superior she felt. And it was not merely social: she made it clear that she knew she had a better mind than anyone around.

The other trouble was, her mind was really quite ordinary.

But, duty done, Randolph could have fun.

'And who do you expect to support you?'

'Luke Fossett, for one.'

'The secretary? But it was the secretary's job you were thinking of standing for only a couple of months ago. You said that Luke was useless.'

She brushed this aside with a wave of her spoon, which left red spots like bloodstains over the white tablecloth.

'He's a senior constituency party member. His endorsement will carry weight. And I think Rebecca Thane will support me.'

Randolph pressed a button.

'She has a first-rate brain, and would be a good person to have,' he said.

Pressing this button never failed to amuse him. His wife was unable to listen to praise of other people, particularly of their brains, without some sort of disclaimer. Sometimes there was a long pause, followed by 'Ye-e-es'; at other times there was a long pause followed by a forthright statement of the person's weak points in Alicia's opinion. Or alternatively there would just be an endless pause.

Tonight, because she wanted to emphasize the strength of her support, Alicia made the pause shorter, followed by: 'She's a very good sort of person,' which in her language was a mild put-down.

Randolph set down his spoon and wiped his mouth.

'I'm not really sure why you're bothering,' he said.

Alicia threw up her chin.

'I'd be a very good councillor.'

'I'd be the last to say you wouldn't.' I wouldn't dare, he

thought to himself. 'But what value has the nomination? It may not be true that there's no safe Conservative seat in the country, but I'd say it was true that there is no safe Conservative ward in Leeds at the moment.'

Alicia shook her head dismissively.

'Oh, the voters will come back. Conservative Leeds is true blue. All they need is someone who will fight.'

'Oh, you'll fight all right.'

The chin went up again. Then she thought for a moment.

'What I'll need is an issue.'

Randolph Ingram mimed thought.

'All the issues seem to be with the other side at the moment: the privatized water companies, the closing down of Barry Proctor School, the emergency ward closures in Leeds hospitals . . .'

He almost seemed to say all this with relish.

'Don't be so defeatist, Randolph!' She pursed her lips, as she did when she was being crossed. 'Something will come to me. It always does.' She closed her eyes for a moment or two. 'Hasn't someone said something about a hostel for druggies?'

A boy who had come to the refuge the night before was proving a problem. Young man, rather. He was very large, but not in a physically threatening way. He was six feet tall, but his bulk was largely fat, and he made no aggressive gestures. Even Katy felt no nervousness about being alone with him. The amount he had eaten at supper – and he would have eaten more if there had been more – had shown how the fat had accumulated. While forking it in he had said that his name was Simon, but that was the only thing he said. He had shown no interest in the talk going on around him – the talk of the day's events, of the dossers and drunks known to all those who sleep rough, of police tactics that for some was harassment, for others an elaborate and good-natured game. He had sat dull-eyed through all that. Afterwards he had gone up to his bedroom (which was the biggest bedroom in number twenty-two), and apparently had gone

46

straight to bed, because Alan had gone up there to talk to another refugee and had heard snores.

In the morning Ben had talked to him in the hallway, as he was on his way out.

'Do you beg in town?' he asked, in the neutral tones he was so good at.

'Yeah,' mumbled the young man.

'Where's your pitch?'

'Near the station. Don't get much.'

'Oh?'

'They think I'm fat and don't need it. I need it *more*.'

The last was said fiercely. Ben nodded calmly.

'You ought to talk to some of the others about techniques. I think your clothes are too good. It's obvious that you haven't been on the streets long.'

Simon looked down at his oversize coverings – grey flannels, a clean blue hand-knitted pullover, uncracked shoes – with apparently no thought beyond the identifiable one that time would cure that. He turned to go to the door.

'You could help prepare the evening meal this afternoon,' said Ben. Simon stopped with his hand on the knob. 'The food for supper. Peel vegetables, chop up, that kind of thing. I told you about it last night. We start preparing the meal about five.'

There was the faintest of glimmers in Simon's eyes.

'Yeah,' he said. 'Yeah, I'll help.'

But when he came down and settled his bulk on the three-legged stool in the kitchen it was evident he would be no help at all. His mother had obviously done everything for him, making him quite incapable of fending for himself. He was set to peel potatoes for the shepherd's pie (and a great number of potatoes needed to be peeled for one of the Centre's shepherd's pies), but he had no idea how to go about it, and more potato seemed to be hacked or scraped on to the newspaper than into the saucepan. Alan tried him on carrots, to no better effect. Then Katy suggested he cut up the braising steak she had cajoled out of the Dewhurst's manager at a knockdown price (he thought she was one of a large family, and would probably have been quite

47

unforthcoming if he had known she was feeding a refuge for the homeless), and then feed it into the hand mincer which Ben had brought along with his own effects to number twenty-four. When this proved to be just about within his power Katy opened the cupboard and took down a packet of custard creams. This was what helping had been all about. For form's sake she put them on a plate, but she and Alan had no more than one each.

'Is this the problem with your family?' she asked. She could not yet manage the neutral tones that Ben did so well.

'What?'

'Eating?'

'Yeah.'

She tried again.

'Were they trying to get you to slim?'

'Yeah . . . That and the cost.'

'Didn't you have a job?'

He shook his head slowly.

'Never had a job. Mum's just a housewife, and Dad's a caretaker. Not much money coming into the house. Then the doctor said I ought to slim, and they started laying down rules.'

Ben had been doing work on the plumbing in number twenty-two – he was a supremely handy odd-job man. Now he came in, stood in the kitchen doorway and said: 'Wouldn't it be better to obey the rules than live rough on the streets?'

'Yeah,' said Simon slowly. 'But there were other things.'

And with that gnomic utterance they had to be content. The set of the body was one they all knew, it said he would answer no more questions. Ben will find out eventually, thought Katy. When Simon had finished feeding the mincer with chopped meat, he took the last couple of biscuits and sloped off to his bedroom without another word.

Most of the people in the refuge had changed by now, though Tony, the young boy, had been given an extra week's grace, because Ben was hopeful he could get him to go back to his parents' home. Bett Southcott had been and come back, more willing to help this time: Ben's policy of patience and quiet sympathy seemed to be paying off in her case. They had a new dog – Queenie, a humorous jet-black mongrel, the pet or friend of a girl who called herself Jezebel. There was also an undersized, rat-like person with vicious eyes, who smelled. His name was Mouse. Katy had to keep telling herself that there weren't many like him. Jezebel was a jolly, uncomplicated girl whose very nickname was a humorous gesture. She kept the supper table lively, and Queenie made for conversation with her variety of begging techniques.

'You could learn from her,' said Ben to Simon.

He looked down with his dull eyes at the funny black face, not seeming to comprehend.

After supper Jezebel and Tony washed up, and Alan put away. There was chaos if the washers-up were allowed to put away – things would go missing for days. That was the last duty of the day, however. Once or twice, on fine evenings, Alan and Katy had gone with Ben to the pub and sat outside with a soft drink. They were never quite sure that they were welcome, though, and they were unused to pubs. They told themselves that, after all, they had been together, the three of them, all day. Tonight Ben just said he was off for a pint, and they respected his privacy. He had been on duty since before breakfast time, with odd jobs, shopping, and a long confessional session with Bett Southcott. Alan and Katy settled down to a game of Scrabble, sometimes interrupted by people coming down for a mug of coffee, or their having to get up to shout up the stairs to tell someone to turn their tranny down. The Centre was never entirely quiet until about midnight, but most of the noises were expected and comfortable.

They were getting into a routine – a routine that would have been unimaginable only a few weeks before. Sometimes Alan and Katy felt like pinching themselves to make sure their new life wasn't a dream.

It was coming up to ten o'clock, and they were watching a feeble sitcom on television, when the front door bell rang. Alan pressed the mute button and went out to the front door. Katy, impelled by she knew not what except that she thought it was a female voice, went to the hall door to listen. Whoever she was, she was urgent, impassioned. Katy went out into the hall, then to the front door to stand beside Alan.

'I've told her there's no room,' Alan said, turning to her.

The girl outside was brown-skinned, dark-eyed, and very beautiful. She looked about seventeen, and was carrying a small suitcase. She was clean, almost well dressed, in the Western manner, and she did not look like a candidate for the Centre.

'Please. *Please*. You've got to help me,' she said, her black eyes turning to Katy. 'My father is trying to force me to marry a terrible man. A horrible person, someone I hate more than I can explain. I'd commit suicide rather. If I sleep rough my father will find me. I would stand out. If I go to relatives they'll send me back home. Please! Please help me!'

Katy's decision was immediate.

'You can sleep with me in my room,' she said, standing aside. 'Tomorrow we'll talk it over with Ben. He'll know what to do.'

CHAPTER 6

Sanctuary

Katy and Alan made no bones about it: they were not going to wait up for Ben, not going to ask his permission. By the morning he could be presented if not with a *fait accompli* then at least with a situation that would seem to have been temporarily solved.

It was not that they mistrusted Ben, doubted his sympathy or compassion. They knew him, their newly discovered father, or thought they did. His instinct would be to offer the girl the protection of the Centre. On the other hand, they remembered the note of caution he had sounded after his talk with Dickie Mavors: they had to be more careful who they took in. And there was no doubt that the newcomer fell well outside the usual category of young people for whom the refuge was set up.

Her name was Mehjabean Haldalwa, but she said she was known at school as Midge. That Katy found out, and much more, as they talked before sleeping together in the three-quarters bed in her room. Her father was Razaq Haldalwa and he owned five corner shops in the Kirkstall and Head-ingly districts of Leeds, staffed by relatives of varying degrees of closeness. In general it did not seem that Midge was afraid of her father, or was anything other than affectionate and respectful. His, however, was a success story that had gone sour, especially since the supermarkets were by law allowed to open on Sundays. It was her father's financial predicament that was behind Midge's present plight. Three months before she had been a schoolgirl without a care in the world – beyond, that is, passing exams, finding a university course that might lead to actually finding a job, and all the other areas of anxiety that Katy and Alan were similarly aware of.

The question was, how to break the news to Ben, and this was the subject of many looks and whispers as Alan and Katy went about their early-morning chores.

'Ben, we had a new one come last night,' Alan finally said, as, all three in the kitchen, they made the breakfast toast and tea. Alan tried to keep his tone light, as Ben usually did when talking to the young people at the refuge, but all the same Ben looked up from his buttering of toast.

'I thought we were full. Did somebody take off?'

'No . . . It was a bit of an emergency.' Under Ben's bland gaze he stammered a little. 'It's . . . it's this Indian girl.'

'Pakistani,' said Katy quietly.

'Yes. Pakistani . . . She's being forced by her father to marry a man she hates. She came here to sort of hide . . .'

He stumbled to a stop. Ben's look became thoughtful.

'There's refuges for people in that sort of situation. I'm pretty sure there's one in Bradford. I wonder how I could get a telephone number for them. Obviously they won't be in the book. They have to be *there* for women, but keep themselves quiet, which must be a bit of a problem.'

Alan and Katy breathed a tentative sigh of relief.

'But you won't turn her out?'

Ben shook his head without hesitation.

'No, of course not. But we must face the fact that this is not the best place for her. It's the same with her as with addicts. Better for the girl herself and better for us if we can find somewhere where there are people with experience of this particular problem, people with the tools to help her.'

Alan looked surreptitiously at Katy, and they both nodded.

Later on, Mehjabean came down. Katy had arranged it like that so that they had a chance to soften Ben up first. Only she didn't put it like that to Midge, and she didn't even put it like that to herself, for she had an enormous respect for Ben, even as she was a mite sceptical about his treatment of the obvious skivers and bludgers. Midge came into the kitchen, smiled at Ben, then she and Katy set to to make more toast and marmalade and strong coffee, which she said was *her* drink. Then they all sat around the battered old table.

'So your family is trying to pressure you into a marriage you don't want, is that right?' Ben opened gently.

Midge's eyes glinted. When she looked like that she didn't seem like a Midge at all, but very much a Mehjabean.

'Not pressure – *force*. My father is in debt to this . . . this man, this *horrible* man, and this is his way of getting him to cancel it.' She shook her head, her mouth set firm. 'I would never have believed it of him, never.'

'It doesn't sound like the usual Asian marriage,' commented Ben. 'Seems like it's the wrong way round.'

Mehjabean nodded.

'It is. But he wants *me*. And this is his way of getting me – of *buying* me. He doesn't mind if I'm reluctant – that gives it more spice for him. It's not my father's fault . . . No, that's not true: of course it's his fault, of course he should not think of selling his daughter to a repulsive old lecher. But he is under a lot of pressure. It's not just him and us: it's the whole large family, people who depend on him for a not very good living. The longer I can remain vanished, the more I can escape the pressures from him and them, and the more he'll be forced to find another way out of his difficulties.'

'Yes, I can see that,' Ben said, his face screwed up in contemplation. 'How did you get to hear about us?'

'From a schoolfriend. She was on the streets for a bit, when her mum had a new boyfriend who was harassing her.'

'You know, don't you, that we're a refuge for the homeless –'

'I am homeless!'

'In a sense.' Ben hadn't lost his cool. 'But we're really for young people who have been on the streets for a while.'

'If I sleep rough, my father will find me.'

'What I'm saying is that there are places for people in your situation. I'm pretty sure there's one in Bradford for Asian women who are being pressurized into unwanted marriages or fleeing from unhappy ones.'

The glint was now steely in Midge's eye.

'I am not an Asian woman. I am a British woman who happens to be brown-skinned and Moslem. If I *am* a Moslem.'

'I think you know what I mean, Midge.'

His calmness and persistence lowered the temperature, as it usually did.

'Yes, I know what you mean. But can you see it from my point of view? *Try*! Why should I be compartmentalized, made into a typical problem of my community?'

'Well, there aren't many white British girls who are forced into marriage these days.'

It was said lightly. Midge saw the joke, and grinned.

'I suppose what you're really saying is that I'm a bit of an embarrassment to you in the work you're trying to do.'

Ben didn't try any facile denial.

'A bit of a problem, anyway. Something we're not really used to. And you could give a handle to people who will use any ammunition they can get against us.'

'I can't see how giving protection to someone like me could provide ammunition for anyone.'

'No. How could it?' put in Katy loyally.

Ben explained patiently.

'Anything involving the ethnic minorities can be sensitive. There's the point too that other places, like the Bradford refuge, can offer you much better advice than we can. They'll have specialist people there, or at any rate on call. That's what you need – people to tell you your legal rights, to tell you what, with all their experience, is the best way of fighting this thing. Experience tells, you know.'

'Ye-e-es.'

'Look, I'll try to find out their number, and then we can at least make contact with them. Remember, there's a fortnight limit on stays here, and I can't see why we should make an exception for you.'

There was a pause. Mehjabean's incipiently beautiful face registered the pressures of differing emotions and impulses. Finally she said: 'All right.' All of them conscious that she didn't have a great deal of choice. She knew they would not want to throw her out, but equally she knew she needed to retain Ben's goodwill.

Getting in touch with the refuge for Asian women proved not to be child's play. Ben remembered a journalist contact

54

on the *Bradford Telegraph and Argus*, but when he finally
found him at his desk the man was adamant that the phone
number was something that simply was not given out, not
even to a trusted friend. Ben kept his cool, and finally the
man came up with a compromise.

'Look, the number's sacrosanct, just as the address is. You
don't have to be Albert Einstein to guess why. But I'll give
them your number and get them to call you. I'll tell them
you've got a pretty urgent problem – they're run off their
feet as a rule, but they are eager to help anyone in that
situation, and I'm sure they'll get back to you as soon as they
can.'

So they had to be content with that.

It meant that Ben had to potter around number twenty-
four all day, doing a succession of non-urgent jobs. Alan and
Katy recognized that he was the one who would have to
handle the matter, though they hoped they would be allowed
to have an input in any decision. It was clear that Mehjabean
intended to have an input too. She stayed around on the
ground floor for that purpose, but making herself very useful.
It was remarkable, but fortunate too, that the girl faced with
this sort of threat should be such a formidable individual.
She and Ben talked a lot during the day, on neutral topics
mostly, and really got to know each other. She promised to
teach Katy and Alan to make an elementary and non-time-
consuming sort of curry. They wondered whether the
Centre's inmates would like curry, but Midge said that everyone liked curry these days, and they'd certainly like hers.
On reflection Alan and Katy realized that curry and rice
would save some of the time spent on peeling vegetables.

The call came from the refuge for Asian women towards
five o'clock. It was Ben who took it.

'Good of you to ring,' he said. Then, courtesies over, he
began to summarize the case.

'The situation is this. We run a short-term hostel for
kids on the streets. Unofficial. Last night we had someone
come who's outside our normal categories. She's an Asian
girl who's being strongly pressurized by her family to marry
a much older man whom she loathes. It's not a problem,

55

frankly, that we know how to handle.' It was good that Ben could not see Mehjabean's face at this point. She did not like being discussed as a problem. 'We wonder', he went on, 'whether you could take her on, and her case.'

The reply went on for some time. His face fell as he listened.

'Could you put her on the waiting list then? . . . Weeks, I see . . . No, as far as I can tell there's no family member that she could go to. They're part of the pressure, in fact . . . It's not just a question of giving her somewhere to stay – not primarily that, in fact. It's getting her good advice. She hasn't much idea about her rights, and the truth is, we haven't much either . . . Stay put, simply refuse to go with him. Yes, that makes sense. What about the legal aspect?'

It was at that point in the conversation that Ben's face began to brighten up. He took a ball pen from his pocket and reached for a pad from the shelf under the telephone.

'So we can have her name and number, can we? She's just a normal solicitor, right . . . Yes, I've got that. And her telephone number? Well, that is a help. A big help. And, just in case the thing hasn't worked itself through to a solution, if you could add her name to the waiting list. Mehjabean Haldalwa . . . I really am very grateful to you.'

He put the phone down.

'I am not a problem,' said Mehjabean.

'OK, OK,' said Ben calmly. 'You're not a problem, you're a person. Don't get on your high horse. Actually you're a problem *and* a person. A lot of people are. Let's not quarrel, and let's try to solve the problem that you have – right?'

Midge nodded. It had really been no more than a formal protest.

'You probably got the gist of that. Places at the refuge are at a premium – there's a long waiting list. What the poor women do while they're waiting I can't imagine. Anyway, she's given me the name of a solicitor who has special expertise in this kind of case. I'll give her a ring tomorrow. Meanwhile she says stay put, resist any pressure on you to go back to your family –'

'What if the pressure is force – physical force?' demanded Mehjabean

Ben thought.

'We'll just have to keep the doors locked day and night and be very careful who we open the door to. Careful about keys too . . . I wonder if we ought to inform the police too. They might turn out to be on your side, and they might be a help if there was any question of force being used by your family.'

'D C Peace was pretty helpful and sympathetic in our case,' put in Alan. 'You might be able to ring him up and talk to him – privately, as it were.'

'Good idea. Do you think he could be tactful as well as sympathetic?'

'Could be, I should think. Pretty frightening, if necessary, too.'

'I was wondering about a *warning* to Midge's father, not to try anything. That might pay dividends.'

Katy was standing by the windows, glad that the thing was being discussed and that Ben was not just handing down a decision. She wished she had more of a contribution to make, over and above her great wish to have her new friend stay long, as long as she needed, forever, maybe. Idly her eyes took in things happening in the street outside: two children playing in the front garden, a woman shouting to another woman across the street. There was an Asian man talking to the householder in the pokey pre-war semi just across the way. But though Katy had registered that Bramsey was a predominantly white part of Leeds, she did not realize how rare an Asian visiting a Bramsey home was, so she didn't mention what she had seen till much later.

CHAPTER 7

Closing In

A meeting with the solicitor was easy to arrange. Ben simply rang up next morning and fixed a time with her for late afternoon. The woman was English, but she had a partner from the Pakistani community.

'She doesn't want to spend her life on Asian women's problems,' she said, 'but she's here if we need her – if there's anything in the case I don't quite understand.'

'It seems a fairly straightforward matter,' said Ben, trying to avoid using the word 'problem'.

'Nothing is that, when you have a clash of cultures – different values, different expectations. But I've had enough experience by now to avoid most of the pitfalls. See you at four.'

So that seemed to all of them hopeful.

Mehjabean was going down well in the refuge. Though her clothes alone showed she was not in the usual category of youngsters staying there, no one asked questions; they accepted her, just as most of them accepted the existence of the Centre without asking how or why. She was beautiful, she was smart, she was different. These things in themselves were sufficient to make most of the rest happy and pleased to have her around. She talked a lot, and laughed, and generally brightened up the atmosphere. Katy thought she was wonderful, and she was not the only one. Even Bett Southcott came out of her shell and had a long conversation with Midge over the washing up. And Zak, coming back with Pal after a fortnight sleeping rough, could hardly take his eyes off her.

Mehjabean put on her smartest clothes to go and see the solicitor. She was going to an interview with a professional person, and it seemed natural to her to do so – as it would not so long ago have seemed natural to a white English person to put on his or her best in the same situation. Ben had paint on his trousers and a fleck of white in his rich auburn hair which looked rather distinguished until you realized what it was. Mehjabean was too polite to make any comment. At a quarter to four they left number twenty-four, walked to Ben's five-year-old red Cortina, and drove off. Neither of them was conscious of being watched, but watched they were.

The meeting with the solicitor, overshadowed though it was by what happened later, was useful. Sally Short was cool, practical and experienced. She could tell Midge what her rights were, what had worked well in the past with other and similar cases, what had seemed sensible but had proved counter-productive to the person under pressure. She suggested that, without imprisoning herself, Midge should avoid going out alone, should as far as possible disappear, so as to give her family time to think things through. When she discussed the law it was as a last resort, but she did think a talk with a friendly policeman could only be helpful. Forcing someone of Mehjabean's age and circumstances to go home was something the police were most unlikely to attempt.

Both Ben and Midge were feeling happier on the drive home. They talked about getting in touch with Charlie Peace, keeping within the protective shell of the refuge, and what Midge could do for the place while she was there. She claimed to be a dab hand with the sewing machine, and she pointed out that most of the rooms in the Centre either had no curtains or leftover ones from the previous occupants. It had not been a high priority hitherto, but the need for greater privacy made efficient curtaining desirable. Ben thought he could run to several yards of cheap material.

They had to park the car two or three doors down from number twenty-four, and they got out still talking and laughing.

Before they had got to the gate of the Centre they had

been intercepted by a large, threatening shape, and Midge felt a strong familiar hand gripping her shoulder, though it was Ben whom her father was shouting at.

'Who are you, eh? What you do with my daughter? Why you take her away from her family?'

As she struggled, Midge heard Ben's voice come, cool and calm:

'Mr Haldalwa? Would you let go of your daughter, please. I haven't taken Mehjabean away from her family. I run a refuge for homeless youngsters, and Mehjabean came here two nights ago for protection –'

'My daughter is not homeless! She not need protection!'

Ben's voice stayed calm and level.

'I think she does need protection. Mr Haldalwa, will you let go of your daughter?' At that moment, as Midge made an almighty twist that occupied her father's whole attention, Ben brought his hand down in a karate chop on his arm that had Razaq Haldalwa bellowing with pain, so that by the time he had got control of himself again, Midge and Ben were both within the protection of the Centre and listening to him banging with his good arm on the locked door.

Once inside, Ben lit a rare cigarette, told Katy to put on the kettle, patted Midge encouragingly on the shoulder, then went back to the hall and took up the telephone.

'Is that police headquarters? I'd like to speak to D C Peace if he's there.'

By the time he was talking to Charlie, who was promising to come round as soon as he could get away, the banging on the front door had stopped and he had heard the gate click.

Dickie Mavors was not used to dealing with people who were not English by birth and white by colour. He was perfectly amiable, in a benign, old-chappish sort of way, but faced with the rage of Razaq Haldalwa he felt himself to be distinctly at a loss, sometimes speechless, sometimes deciding he had to interrupt the flow of outrage when he caught some words that seemed to promise stepping-stones through a flood.

'Your daughter, you say? How old is she?'

It was when the interview – or audience – had been going for some ten minutes that he caught a word that interested him.

'– he says he runs a refuge, what for my daughter needs a refuge, she has good home –'

'Refuge, did you say, old chap? Now would that be the place in Portland Terrace?'

'Yes, Portland Terrace. I go there, I see them together, is not good house, very old –'

Dickie raised a finger.

'Now, I'll tell you who to go and see. One of our very active local workers – could be the next councillor for Bramsey. Her name is Ingram, Alicia Ingram. She's been very concerned about this refuge, and I know she'll be interested in your story. Now, I'll give you her address . . .'

When he had gone, Dickie Mavors, who was never backward in self-congratulation, awarded himself a double measure, and a malt Scotch to boot.

Charlie was round at the refuge less than half an hour after their phone call. He greeted Alan and Katy as old friends, and they introduced him to Ben and Mehjabean. Sparks of fellow-feeling flashed between him and her – two strong, resilient, satiric spirits. But then Charlie sat at his ease in one of the old armchairs and let them tell him the whole story in their own way. Mehjabean's account of the pressure put on her was restrained, but the strength of her feeling showed through. At the end Charlie sat thoughtful for a minute or two.

'I'm not going to pretend it's an easy matter,' he said at last. 'We're into all sorts of grey areas here – and not offending the "ethnic minorities" is just one of them.' He turned to Midge. 'Don't you just love being an ethnic minority?'

'I'd hate to be a boring old majority,' she said. 'Though I hate being lumped together with everyone like me, like when people talk about "Pakistani women", as if we were all alike.'

'Well, at least no one assumes you're a potential mugger,' countered Charlie. 'Anyway, I'm not disguising it would be easier if you were a bit older, if you were white or Afro-Caribbean, and so on. There's definitely a limit to what we can do.'

'The first thing you can do is register the problem – register the situation,' said Ben.

'I do, I do. And I'll pass the information on.'

'We're just terrified that she'll be . . . like, *taken*,' said Katy. Charlie nodded.

'I can see you must be. At least you can get straight through to me if that happens . . . Somehow I don't see her as being easily taken,' he added, and the spark flew between them.

'I won't,' said Midge.

'On the other hand, her father is forceful and strong,' put in Ben. 'Like I said, I had to use karate on him to get her away. And with other family members to help . . .'

'Of course – I wasn't suggesting you should relax for one moment. I agree with all your solicitor's advice, but the fact that you've got people coming and going all the time here can't make things easy.'

'We've thought of giving everyone a key with strict instructions –'

'Keys can be duplicated, and poor people can be bribed,' Charlie pointed out forcefully. 'People come back here for their mail, don't they?'

'Yes, and it's an address they give the DSS.'

'Do they have keys?'

'No-o,' said Ben. 'But some have gone missing, so some of them probably do.'

'I think for the moment, whenever possible, you should keep the place locked, and have all the residents let in as they come home. Withdraw all keys, and have a chain put up. That means a doorman must be here all the time. Not ideal, but you can explain to them why.'

'Yes, we can,' said Alan. 'Most of them are very sympathetic and interested in Midge. We've always had the place open during the day before, but they'll understand.'

'Right,' said Charlie, getting up. 'Well, it looks like you have a meal to cook, so I won't keep you.' He turned towards

Ben. 'Do you think I could have a few words with you alone, sir?'

Ben nodded, and, watched by the other three, they went out to the hall and then in to the dining room. Ben gestured with his hand and they sat at one of the tables already set for supper. Charlie took in the thick, healthy mass of hair, the far-seeing blue eyes, the youthful, almost handsome set of the face. It was easy to see women falling for him – not just fifteen or twenty years ago, but now. What was less easy was fathoming him. The women who had fallen for him did not seem to have been made particularly happy by him.

'I thought I'd have a word in private,' Charlie explained, 'because I've heard whispers of a campaign getting under way against this place.'

Ben nodded, confidence undimmed.

'I've always known it's inevitable. We'll just have to try and give them no handles to hang the campaign on.'

'That's probably easier said than done. Not all homeless people are angels. I know you try not to take addicts –'

'Not because we're unsympathetic. We just couldn't handle the problems involved.'

'But how can you be sure they're not addicts? You'd hardly want to frisk them every time they come in and out, search their rooms morning and night, inspect them for puncture-marks.'

'No, certainly not,' agreed Ben. 'But though I've no quali-fications or particular experience, I'm not completely naive. I think it would become apparent quite quickly if we had an addict, and then I'd get rid of him, one way or another.'

'Drugs is the obvious handle, and in fact the neighbours have tried that already, as you know. If the campaign gets nowhere on that, it'll be something else.'

'We'll face up to it when we know what it is,' said Ben, with serene confidence. He had said he wasn't naive, but Charlie wasn't so sure. He seemed too able to ignore the wickedness of the world and its ways.

'How did you come to start this place?' he asked.

'I'd always wanted to do something for the homeless. It's a sore on our society. We're just throwing away our young people. When I got a biggish win on the National Lottery, I sank it into this place.'

Charlie's antennae which often told him when people were lying did not twitch. Was it because Ben Marchant was telling the truth, he wondered, or because he had a blandness which neutralized those sensitive little indicators?

'When did you involve your children in what you are doing?' he asked. The googlie did not get beyond Ben's defences.

'Ah – they told you?'

'No. I found out.'

'I didn't decide to involve them. They decided. Working with these young people made me think about myself and my past. I've been pretty thoughtless and irresponsible, especially when I was young. I had this urge to at least get to know my children, and I did a bit of spadework to find out what had happened to their mothers. When I made myself known to them we got on well at once. Naturally they wanted to know what I was doing, and they came here, got interested in it and – well, you know the rest.'

It all sounded so simple, so good. Yet he had charged into two young lives and changed their pattern. Admittedly Katy's was a life whose pattern was unhappy, but Charlie had the impression he would have done the same even if she and her mother were close and devoted. He had made no attempt to contact the mothers before he made himself known to the children. Was he perhaps still 'pretty thoughtless and irresponsible' as he had described his young self? Was he one of those people who obeyed their whims of the moment, irrespective of consequences? Charlie didn't doubt Ben's good intentions. He was less sure of his good sense.

Alicia Ingram was as unused as Dickie Mavors to finding people of Asian extraction on her front doorstep. Instinctively she switched on the manner she used when she went into a corner shop, a manner she thought of as 'being nice to them', but one which in fact suggested her usual pity for people whom she regarded as less intelligent than herself, augmented in such cases by the fact that they were also less English.

'Yes? Is there anything I can do for you?'

'Missis Ingram? Your name is given to me by Mr Mavors.'

Once she got past the pronunciation 'Mavvers', Alicia stiffened. Dickie Mavors was no friend of hers, currently.

'Oh yes.'

'It is my daughter. Very bad things happen to her.' Mr Haldalwa thrust his head forward in outrage. 'She has been taken by man at the refuge in Portland Terrace.'

Alicia relaxed.

'Oh dear. This sounds serious. You had better come in.'

Randolph was out, so she took him into the sitting room. She wondered whether to offer him a drink, but decided it would probably be against his religion, whatever that was. She could decide later whether he was worth making tea or coffee for.

'You say your daughter has been taken by the man running the refuge,' she said in her best constituency MP manner. 'Does that mean she had been sleeping rough?'

'No, no. Nothing of the kind,' said Razaq Haldalwa, very agitatedly. 'My daughter is well brought up girl. Excellent education. Doing very well at school. Beautiful girl.'

'I see. Is she romantically involved with him then? Or helping him with his . . . work?'

'No. It is not like that . . .' But he seemed to be having great difficulty explaining what it was like. 'There was trouble – no, not trouble – disagreement at home.'

This Alicia could understand.

'I see. Teenagers are *always* difficult, aren't they? They think they know everything, when really they know *so* little!'

'Is true. Is very true.'

'So, what was this difficulty about?'

'It was a question of . . . of obedience to her father. To her 'ole family. Not to set up in opposition to us.'

This began to sound less than promising. Alicia was all for dutiful children (her own, from her first marriage, had on the whole done what their mother pushed them into, if only for a quiet life), but somehow this all had the odour of

65

something . . . unEnglish, something that would not translate easily into the sort of political terms Alicia needed – something, in short, not easy to make an issue out of.

'And the matter on which she set herself up in opposition to you all?'

If Mr Haldalwa had had a cloth cap to twist, in the tradition of the working-class lad tongue-tied in the presence of his 'betters', he looked as if he would have twisted it.

'Is marriage. Is question of a husband, of opposition to the husband I have chosen for her.'

'Ah-h-h,' said Mrs Ingram, her spirits falling.

Because if there was one thing unlikely to rally the citizens of Bramsey round a cause it was the sanctity of Asian marriage traditions. Bramsey was white, middle class and permissive, with a fringe that was white, working class and permissive. It was as much as they could do to get their daughters to go through a marriage ceremony at all, let alone force them in their choice of partner. They would have not an ounce of sympathy for Mr Haldalwa in his dilemma. Alicia had a sudden sense that the world of local politics was not a bed of roses, but she squared her shoulders.

'We must see what we can do,' she said.

CHAPTER 8

Violent Ends

The trouble, when it erupted, started with the boy called Mouse. This was the undersized, vicious-looking young man who had been getting more and more difficult each day, and was now nearing the end of his fortnight. His name, obviously, was ironic, and his rat-like nature had become ever more apparent. Mehjabean had seemed to act as some kind of catalyst. Though he occasionally used the word 'Paki', the problem didn't seem to be mainly racial: he seemed to resent her nice clothes, her loveliness, the fact that she was welcome, admired, almost loved in the refuge. The sight of the others laughing with her, confiding in her, sent him off into spasms of sneering or rage. It was the darkness gazing at light, and not being able to bear the brightness.

Ben took on the job of telling him that when his time was up he wouldn't be welcome at the Centre in future.

'What the fuck you mean?' demanded Mouse, his face tilted up aggressively at Ben's.

'I mean you haven't fitted in well here,' said Ben quietly. Mouse's face twisted in derision.

'Fitted in! Is this the fucking boy scouts, then? Nobody told me I had to fit in.'

'If this place is to have any future at all,' said Ben, always quiet, 'it has to have a pleasant atmosphere that young people will want to come into.'

'*Well?*'

'Your getting at people the whole time is unhelpful.'

'Who's getting at people?'

'You. And there's another thing: we have to be very careful

here at the moment. There are people watching us who are just looking for an excuse to have us closed down. Your sort of unpleasantness can lead to feuds, fights, anything. I'm surprised it hasn't already. People don't like to be niggled, narked the whole time. I'm not going to take the risk. Until I'm quite sure your attitude has changed you won't be welcome back here.'

'Well, goodbye Mary Poppins,' said Mouse. 'Pardon me if I fart.' He spat on the threadbare hall carpet and went up to his little bedroom in the attic, where he proved his attitude had not changed by scrawling graffiti directed at Ben and Mehjabean on the walls – graffiti that included plenty of four-letter words, including the word 'kill'. To be precise, the phrase that stood out, because he'd done it as a two-colour affair in large capitals, was 'KILL THE FUCKING DO-GOODER AND HIS TART'. When his dirty and holed rucksack had been stuffed full of his possessions he kicked open the door of his room and made his way down to the first-floor landing.

Downstairs in the hall Ben had just answered the phone.

'Oh yes – Mrs Ingram. I know the name . . . and yes, I had heard of your concern . . . I assure you . . . Mrs Ingram, the police have been here, they have searched the place for drugs, and they're perfectly satisfied . . . I do think the police are the people best qualified to conduct a drugs search, don't you? . . .' (Ben's tone was impeccably diplomatic, and he managed to maintain it where other people might have let show that it was wearing thin. Up on the landing Mouse stirred, interested.) 'I'm happy to talk to you any time, Mrs Ingram. I'm sure you support anything that helps the homeless, don't you? . . . But most of the people here have no home to go back to . . .'

Mouse had heard enough. He dived into his belongings, retrieved a package, and tucked it behind an old chest of drawers that stood by the wall of the landing. Then he struggled down the stairs, rucksack bumping on the bannisters, and as he passed Ben in the hall he aimed a vicious kick at his ankles, which he diverted at the last moment to connect with the leg of the telephone table. It must have sounded like a shot at the other end.

'Sorry, Mrs Ingram. Something fell over,' said Ben, as the front door banged. 'You were saying?'

What Mrs Ingram was saying was that she thought she ought to come round to the – what was it called? – to the *Centre* to talk to him, that she couldn't say when that would be because she'd have to consult her diary, but it was probably best for her visit to be unprepared for, wasn't it, so that she could see the refuge as it *really* was . . .

It was all said in the manner of a school matron planning an unscheduled raid on the dorms. It was also vaguely insulting, though voiced with a blithe disregard for the implications of what she said. Ben was momentarily wrong-footed, failed to question what right she had to inspect or judge, and fell into some cliché about having 'nothing to hide'. There was silence at the other end, which enabled him to right himself. He said: 'I shall look forward to seeing you,' and put the phone down.

But he was worried. He stood for a few moments in the hall, thinking over the conversation he had just had. What if Mrs Ingram came while he was out, and talked to Alan or Katy? There was no teenager on earth capable of the tact and self-restraint that a sparring match with Mrs Ingram's type called for. He had known women like her all his life: single-minded, persistent, but not very bright. If he was not mistaken the woman's whole endeavour would be for her own advantage or advancement – whether material, psychological or social. A phrase from his childhood schoolbooks came to his mind: 'The creature hath a purpose, and its eyes are bright with it . . .' Keats, was it? He thought he had heard that destructively selfish purpose getting from the eyes to the voice in the conversation he had just had. And it was a voice he could have sworn he had heard somewhere before, or one very like it, though probably it was years and years ago. Ben's had been a picaresque life in his early years, and on his travels the pattern had been to leave people behind rather than take them with him.

'No, not like that.' He heard Katy's clear, teenage voice

from the kitchen. He shook himself free of reminiscent thought and went through to find her trying to stop Simon carving up and throwing away most of the runner beans he was stringing. Simon himself did not show any sign of shame at his total lack of domestic skills, but when Katy tried to show him how to string them without ruining most of the bean itself, he suddenly said:

'I can hoover.'

They were so surprised at him offering even the most trivial information about himself that they could not believe their ears.

'I beg your pardon?' Kay said.

'I can hoover. I always did the hoovering at home.'

'Well,' said Ben, 'why don't we set you on to giving the whole place a good hoovering over?'

Even he, so skilled in getting the right tone, was unable to keep a trace of false heartiness out of his voice. But when they got out the vacuum cleaner and plugged it in, Simon showed there was something he could use his bulk for: starting in the dining room he gave the place a thorough going-over, moving the furniture with ease, getting into corners, adjusting the suction for obdurate bits. Ben raised his eyebrows at Katy, and they smiled at each other: another problem solved.

'Can I come in?'

Mr Haldalwa's reception of him at the front door had been far from friendly, but Charlie Peace was used to that. Flourishing his ID under his eyes and insisting that he read it had resulted in some modification of his hostility.

'Of course, of course. You come through, Mr Peace.'

The hallway was wide. The semi that the Haldalwas lived in was large and distinctly upmarket: the part of Headingly they had chosen would certainly not have given them many Asian neighbours. It was a house of someone who was doing well in the world, or who had been doing well.

If he did not have Asian neighbours, he certainly had family. When Charlie was ushered into the living room he found, seated on armchairs and the chairs from the dining table, ten or twelve people, the women in saris, most of the men in Western dress or a modified form of it. They all looked at him dark-eyed, saying nothing. This must be Midge's extended family. There were lots of things to be said in favour of the extended family, but at the moment Charlie couldn't think of any of them.

'I was hoping for a word with you in private,' he said, turning to the head of the family.

'You talk before these people. Are all family members. We here to talk family matters. No secrets here.'

'Very well . . .' But it was difficult to frame the warning he wanted to give Mr Haldalwa before so many veiled, unwelcoming eyes. Charlie ignored the offer of a chair and stood, looking at Razaq Haldalwa alone. 'Mr Haldalwa, I gather you made an attempt to bring your daughter Mehjabean back home by force yesterday. If you repeat that attempt you could be – *would* be – in very serious trouble. Let me spell that out: depending on what charge we decided to bring, you could be facing a considerable jail sentence. I hope I make myself clear?'

There was a moment's pause, then Mr Haldalwa spread out his hands ingratiatingly. He was not, Charlie guessed, a cruel or tyrannical man, merely one under pressure. But ingratiating himself was part of his way of life, and he naturally resorted to this mode in the present situation.

'You're taking this too serious, Mr Peace, much too serious. This is just a little family dispute.'

'That would make no difference to the charge.'

Mr Haldalwa rubbed his hands.

'It's what they call a clash of cultures, eh? Different peoples, different ways of going about things. You must know that from your own life, Mr Peace.'

Charlie held him in his gaze.

'If you mean that I think and react the same as if I'd been brought up in Jamaica, then you're wrong, Mr Haldalwa. I don't, because I was brought up in London. I relate more easily to other Londoners than I do to Jamaicans. And Mehjabean's been brought up in Leeds. Some of her ideas are your ideas, but a lot of them aren't.'

'You know my daughter?'

'I've talked with her.'

'Is it wrong to expect a child to honour her parents?'

'No.'

'To follow her parents' wishes?'

'Yes, it is, if they conflict with strong feelings of her own. Look – I'm not going to argue this clash of cultures thing with you, Mr Haldalwa, especially when I'm badly out-numbered. I'm only interested in the law, and seeing it's obeyed, right? And if you don't leave your daughter to sort out her own wishes and feelings, then you'll be in deep trouble.'

Mr Haldalwa shook his head.

'You make too much of it, Mr Peace. I only wanted to talk to her. Tell her she was being silly, that I would never force her into a marriage that she didn't want.'

'Hmmm. That wasn't what it sounded like.'

'I tell you, is all at an end. Mr Siddiq, he withdrew. Mehja-bean, she can go on with school and university.'

This was an item of news that was proffered very late in the conversation. Charlie mistrusted it.

'All that you must work out with her. Perhaps you could find some third party to arbitrate. I wouldn't recommend her to come home before the situation is very, very clear. Meanwhile, if there is any attempt to force her back, force her into marriage, by *anyone* –' he looked around the assembled family, particularly at the men, stern, blank-eyed – 'then we will come down on that person very, very hard. I hope that is understood.'

There was silence – not a flicker of a response. As Charlie turned and made his way down the hallway he decided that he didn't know what effect those family members would have on Mehjabean, but by God they terrified him.

Ben had rather thought that Mrs Ingram would leave little time before paying the threatened visit. She had given the impression even over the phone of a woman who would not let the grass grow under her feet – or, to put it less politely, her voice suggested a woman who, once she had got an idea, would charge ahead with it without thought of the consequences. Since she had also given the impression of being sophisticated yet unsubtle, he had to acquit her of any charge that she had deliberately chosen the worst possible time. Yet that, coincidentally, was when she came, on the evening of the day she had telephoned.

There had been a knock on the door at the end of supper. Rather expecting a Conservative lady, Laura Ashley in dress and bossy of manner, Ben, when he opened it, had been confronted by a fleshy Asian who seemed to be in an attitude of propitiation that did not come naturally to him.

'Mr Marchant? Don't shut the door. There won't be no trouble from me. I just want a little word with Mehjabean.'

Ben stood four-square.

'I'm afraid we have already had trouble with people who say they just want a word with Mehjabean.'

'Her father very sorry about that. He's had a visit from a policeman and it won' happen again. This is different. I'm Mehmet Siddiq. Mehjabean may have told you my name. I want to tell her all this stuff is at an end. No more question of marriage. I withdraw. Is over.'

Ben nodded, standing his ground.

'I see. Well, that's somethin' I can tell her –'

'If I can just have a moment – tell her I'm sorry –'

But his voice and accent had penetrated through to the dining room where the Centre's residents were still sitting around after supper, and it was not difficult for them to guess that some further harassment of Midge was in the offing. First out into the hall was Zak with Pal, and both went to stand beside Ben.

'You get away from here, you old fart. Midge don't want nowt to do wi' you.'

Pal's bark was not the bark of a watchdog or guard dog, but – infected by the general hostility – he did his best. By now the hallway was filling up with a motley and ragged army of defenders, and Mr Siddiq took a step backwards, down on to the front path, from where he had to look up at Ben and his supporters, putting him further at a disadvantage.

'Look, I don' want trouble. You just tell Mehjabean –'

There was jeering from the hallway. Mr Siddiq turned, and as if on some theatrical cue there appeared at the gateway that Laura Ashley-clad figure that Ben had expected earlier, hands on the gate, looking at the scene with an expression of feigned shock and barely concealed pleasure. Mr Siddiq turned back to the faces opposing him.

'You tell her. You tell her is all over.'

Then he brushed past Mrs Ingram and hurried towards his car. There was silence from the refuge. Visitor and visited looked at each other, neither attracted by the sight. When Alicia spoke it was in the hushed and carefully articulated tones that Mrs Thatcher used to use in interviews when she wanted to be most threatening.

'Obviously I've come at an inconvenient time. I'll be back when things are more . . . normal.'

To Alan, standing behind Ben's shoulder and watching this second visitor also retreating to her car, there had been an oddity in the woman's words. She had paused before the final word, and if he'd merely heard her he would have thought she was searching for that last word. But looking at her as well she seemed to him to be momentarily nonplussed by something she had seen. Some*one* she had seen, perhaps? Presumably, therefore, someone standing in the doorway. As they stood there watching the billowing russet tints of her dress as she opened her car door, the telephone rang.

'Right – battle's over!' said Ben, shooing them out of the hall and taking up the handset. It was Charlie Peace.

'Mr Marchant? I thought I'd tell you I've been to talk to Mr Haldalwa.'

'I know.'

'Oh? Has he rung you or been round?'

'No, the suitor has.'

'I see . . .' Ben could sense Charlie considering the implications of this. 'Was it a friendly visit?'

'Yes. At least on the surface. He said he wanted to talk to Mehjabean.'

'Did he?'

'No. I said I'd give her a message.'

'I think that was wise.'

'Then things got rather out of hand. One or two – well, more actually – of the residents came into the hall, and there was some hostility.'

'A fight?'

'Oh no, nothing like that.'

'Then I shouldn't worry too much. I presume he wanted to assure her that she could go back and live with her family.'

'That seemed to be the message. That the marriage was off.'

'Yes, that was the message I was given. I don't know whether I believe it. What are you going to advise her?'

'I don't advise. But we'll talk it over. I don't see any need to rush things myself.'

'Nor do I. I think the important thing is that the terms of her going back are clear to both sides before she actually moves back in with her family. That sounds legalistic, but experience suggests that it's necessary. And it's essential that she gets the terms down on paper.'

'I'll tell her that. Oh, by the way, during the fracas this Mrs Ingram arrived. She seemed to regard it with great satisfaction.'

'I wouldn't worry too much about her. She seems mainly interested in muscling in on any possible local issue in order to get the Conservative nomination for the Bramsey ward.'

'That's what I heard. I'll play it cool. Anyway, thanks a lot for your help.'

'Remember – take care.'

'Oh, I think the battle's over for today.'

But Ben went and checked that the front and back doors were locked.

It was half an hour later, when Mehjabean and Alan were finishing the washing-up, that Ben went into the kitchen, sat on one of the bench-tops and watched them for a moment. As Alan dried the last plate he said:

'I think we should talk, Midge.'

She nodded.

'Sure. About what?'

'It seems as though things are entering a new phase.'

'Maybe . . . But OK, let's talk.'

Ben led the way through to the dining room, and they sat down together on two of the chairs still set around the dining tables. Midge looked enquiringly at Ben, and he thought for the hundredth time what a beautiful woman she was going to be.

'Well, the position seems to be that your father has abandoned this projected marriage,' he said.

'*Seems* to be,' emphasized Midge. Then she conceded: 'It's not impossible. My father has always seemed a fairly reasonable man, until now.'

'And apparently Mr Siddiq has abandoned the idea, too.'

Midge screwed up her face.

'Ye-e-es. I find that even more difficult to judge, because I don't really know him. I don't get the impression he would find it easy to climb down. On the other hand, he may have decided that a forced marriage with a young bride would go down badly with his white British contacts if they got to hear of it.'

'What does he do?'

'Makes cheap clothes. Most of his buyers are white – they're cheap Western-style clothes. He may not want to seem like an ogre or a tyrant to them. Or, more to the point, he may be afraid of appearing ridiculous in their eyes.'

'That was D C Peace on the phone earlier. I brought him up to date and he advised caution.'

'He didn't need to. I'm not rushing into anything.'

'He emphasized that before you go back to live with your family the terms on which you're going back should be clearly agreed, and then put in writing.'

'Yes. Yes, I'm sure that's right. And I'd like to know that my father has solved his financial problems as well . . .' Midge looked down at the table, thoughtful. 'We're not a primitive family, you know. Some girls, in my situation, would be in fear of their lives if they were taken back. That's not the case with me. But constant drips can wear away a stone. That's more what I fear.'

'Yes. Though I think it would need an awful lot of drips.'

She looked up, and shot him a brilliant smile.

'The thing is: is it all right to stay here?'

'I don't see why not. We should probably regard you as a special case. I had my doubts at first, but you don't take up a room, sharing with Katy, and you pull your weight. Everyone likes you, and there are good reasons for relaxing the "fortnight and then out" rule. No, my feeling is that you add generally to the gaiety of nations, or this particular part of this particular nation, and you're welcome to stay on.' He reached over the table and took her hand in his. 'I hope you'll see this as a second home – a home from home. What we have to try and do is make it absolutely safe for you.'

Mehjabean instinctively wanted to nestle her head against his shoulder, as once she used to do with her real father, and she was just wondering whether this would be understood for what it was when there was a sudden irruption from the doorway behind her and she felt a presence over her, then a searing terrible pain down the length of her cheek, and she heard a cry of anguish that was not her own and felt Ben slump, choking and bloody, down on to her lap, and a terrible wetness on her jeans.

Midge clutched him to her and began to scream.

CHAPTER 9

Aftermath

Through the pain Mehjabean heard footsteps in the hall, footsteps stumbling in a rush downstairs, heard the door of the dining room flung open. Then, as she felt Alan's hand on her shoulder, realizing he had taken the choking body of Ben from her lap and was laying it on the floor, she fell forward and found herself being cradled in Katy's arms. There was still noise, more and more footsteps, both on the stairs and from the upper floors. She heard the voice of Alan, now in the hall.

'Stop there! Don't get in the way. Anyone know anything about first aid? Jezebel. Go in and do what you can. I'm ringing for police and ambulance. Zak – get clean towels and cloths. You know where they are . . . ambulance and police – Bramsey area . . . Come quickly . . . there's been a serious attack. You must get him to hospital . . . 24 Portland Terrace . . .'

Mehjabean was conscious of Katy taking her to the ancient sofa in one of the recesses of the dining room, laying her down on it and binding a clean towel around her head, shutting in the searing pain. Katy was still folding it round when a siren was heard from a distance, then screaming tyres outside.

'They can't be here –' Midge began to say, then flinched.

'Don't talk,' said Katy urgently.

The policemen, a uniformed man and a woman, ran up the path to the front door, then through to the dining room, where Jezebel was trying to stem the blood from the retching figure on the floor. The policewoman knelt beside them and added more expert aid, while the policeman radioed through to police headquarters the urgency of the case and the need for an ambulance to get the victim to hospital.

'You got here quickly,' murmured Alan to the kneeling figure of the policewoman, feeling it was a feeble thing to say.

'We were on our way. The ambulance will take a bit longer. DC Peace should be here before long, too. I believe you know him. What about the other one?'

She gestured towards Midge, who was just a bejeaned figure swathed in a towel, indeterminate as to sex.

'It's facial,' Katy said from the sofa. 'She's in a lot of pain. A deep cut down the cheek.'

'Nasty. They'll both have to go to the infirmary.'

Alan went up to the policeman, who had retreated to the front door, which was open.

'There ought to be a guard on Mehjabean at the hospital. She's under threat from her family.'

'Yes. They're aware of that at police HQ. I'm to go with her. Ah, that sounds like an ambulance.'

Alan turned and saw the white vehicle swerving at speed into the Terrace. He looked the other way, to the doorway of number twenty-two, where a little knot of the residents next door had gathered. He gestured to them to keep back, as the ambulance screamed to a halt and two men ran out, bringing a stretcher. The constable directed them through to the dining room, where one close look at Ben was enough.

'Into the ambulance,' said the first of the medical team, and they began the painful process of stretchering him.

'There's another, over there, with bad facial injuries,' said the constable.

'Fight, was it?'

'Not as far as I know. Double attack. I'm told I'm to come with her.'

'I'll come too,' put in Katy.

'No way,' said the constable firmly. 'You might be a complication, if there was trouble from her family.' He went over to Midge. 'Are you all right? Can you walk?'

Midge nodded, and let him help her up and lead her out

79

to the ambulance on his arm. She gazed into the dim recesses of the vehicle, where Ben was being attached to various devices whose purpose she could only guess at.

'Will he be OK?' she asked, painfully articulating the words. The ambulance man shrugged.

'Can't tell. It's serious all right. Can you get up on your own? Right. You sit here, the constable there.' He banged on the window, the back doors were shut automatically, and the ambulance took off, smooth but fast, in the direction of the Leeds General Infirmary.

Alan watched it go, tears in his eyes: it seemed as if he had just lost someone he had only recently found, just started on the road leading out of Eden. For a moment he was in danger of losing the control that thus far had served him so well. He shook himself and put an arm round Katy, who was beside him, hugging her encouragingly. Then they realized that another police car had drawn up several yards down the road, and Charlie Peace was at the gate, taking in the situation with his sharp eyes, and making swift decisions.

'It was at number twenty-four the attack occurred – right?' He came through the gate and looked at the little knot in the next doorway. 'I don't want anyone from twenty-two coming in and complicating matters.' He looked through into the hall and saw the policewoman. 'Will you go next door, keep everyone there till we're ready to talk to them, but report back if there's anything of interest that seems urgent – for example, anything seen through the windows, heard through the walls.'

He came into the hall and stood in the doorway to the dining room, contemplating the blood on the tablecloth, chairs and floor. He looked at Alan and Katy compassionately.

'You can't always tell by the amount of blood,' he said.

'I heard the ambulance man say it was serious,' said Alan, his voice breaking.

'That was Ben, was it?' Alan nodded. 'And what about Midge?'

'It *looked* horrible and deep,' said Katy, trying to repress a shiver. She had always hated the sight of blood. 'But it was just down the cheek.'

'The police were here so quick,' said Alan. 'Perhaps that will save him. They said they were on their way.'

'That's right,' Charlie nodded. 'We had a call.'

'But how could anyone have called before me?'

Charlie held up his hand and went into the hallway. Jezebel was back on the stairway, and so were Zak and Pal, a pathetically young boy, all three watching proceedings in silence. Charlie nodded to them.

'Thank you for keeping out of the way. That's important, as I'm sure you all know, but not everybody does it. Now, will you all go back to your rooms? There'll be a DCI here before long, and then we'll get down to questioning everybody.'

As they turned and grudgingly went back upstairs, Charlie watched them, then came back to the dining-room doorway.

'Before I start questioning people, I need to know what's been happening today. Ben Marchant told me on the phone about the . . . confrontation, shall we call it, on the doorstep with Mr Siddiq and then Mrs Ingram. I'll need to hear more about that. Had anything else happened, any fight, any trouble that Ben involved himself in?'

They didn't need to think.

'He'd told Mouse he had to go, and wouldn't be welcome back,' said Katy. 'He was a troublemaker.'

'Did he go quietly?'

'He went,' said Alan. 'I heard him dragging his rucksack down the stairs. Then there was a sort of *crack*, almost like a shot. I came to the door and looked into the hall. I saw him disappearing out of the front door, and Ben was steadying the telephone table. I think he'd given it an almighty kick. That would figure – it would be like him.'

'I see . . . Ben was actually on the phone?'

'Yes, to Mrs Ingram. That was when she had called him, and said she was going to come round, without notice, and more or less make an inspection.'

'I see. Very interesting. She seems to want to do our job for us. Right – I have something to do. You two go into the other room and hold the fort. No new people to be admitted tonight, obviously.' He looked up the steep flight of stairs. 'Which was this boy Mouse's room?'

'Top floor, far end of the corridor,' said Katy promptly. 'We haven't done it out, or anything.'

'Good,' said Charlie, and watched the pair, touchingly close, leave the grisly scene of the attack and settle down to make coffee in the kitchen. Then he bounded up the stairs, pausing on the dimly lit landing to feel behind the chest of drawers standing between two of the bedroom doors. He took out, unsurprised, a plastic bag containing white powder, and put it carefully into another plastic bag and docketed it. He paused for a moment to take in the feel of the place. Up here was bright with fresh paint, as it was on the ground floor, but here there was a smell – endemic, ineradicable – of unwashed humanity, dirty clothes. It did its best, but the Centre was still of the street, streety.

He turned to the narrow stairwell and went more slowly up the second flight and into Mouse's room. Again he was unsurprised as he surveyed the mingled bile and filth of the slogans decorating the walls. He soon took in the main drift of the filth, and he had, professionally, to wonder whether there was any truth in it, if there was an affair going on between Ben and Mehjabean. On the whole his instinct told him not. On the way downstairs he knocked at one of the bedroom doors on the first floor. Inside were Zak and Jezebel, in a clinch on a capacious armchair, with Queenie watching intently from behind the door and Pal incuriously stretching his length on the rug. He was much more interested in Charlie than the clinch, and made him welcome.

'Was either of you in when the boy Mouse left earlier today?' Charlie asked.

'Yeah,' said Zak. 'I were.'

'Did you talk to him?'

'No, I just 'eard 'im. 'E cum down to this floor, then 'e waited an age, listening to Ben on the phone downstairs. Then 'e went down to the 'all, an' kicked summat on 'is way out. That was expected. That was Mouse. Vicious little toe-rag. 'E's a rotten street beggar, because 'e looks so threatening.'

'That's very useful. Thanks very much.'

And Charlie bounded down into the hall again, consulted his notebook, and took up the phone and dialled.

'Mrs Ingram?'

When Randolph Ingram got home from a quiet couple of pints at the pub, his wife was sitting draped on the sofa, her red hair spread out like a rising sun around her. She had been at a Tory Party recruitment do, but she got up at once and made him his nightcap. This was usually a sign that she had something to communicate. When he was taking the first sip of his Horlicks she sat down again gracefully and said:

'I've been thinking, Randolph –'

'Mmmm?'

'I think I'll go down and see Mother tomorrow for a few days.'

She didn't see his sceptically raised eyebrows.

'Really, Alicia? I thought you'd more or less washed your hands of her. You said beyond a certain point there was nothing you could do, you couldn't be expected to throw your life away when she showed no gratitude, and the kindest thing you could do would be to leave the pair of them alone.'

Alicia sometimes wished her husband did not remember her words so accurately. It was almost as if he made notes.

'I know, but in the end . . . I mean, Carol is quite hopeless as nurse, guardian, warden – whatever you call it – and since I get *no* news from her, I simply can't judge the situation, decide what is required. Let's face it, I just *don't know* how things are.'

'I thought that was how you liked it.'

'You *know* that's not true, Randolph.' She was getting a good colour up, matching her flaming hair. 'I worry terribly! When someone's failing, and wilful, and frankly going funny . . .'

'Your mother knows her own mind, and always has.'

'She just won't acknowledge that other people may know what is best for her.'

'It's something very few people will acknowledge.'

'But if only Carol would –'

She was interrupted by the telephone. For the last few weeks it had been assumed in the Ingram household that telephone calls were for Alicia.

'Leeds 2647936.'

'Mrs Ingram?' A voice she didn't know. London-common she categorized it as in her mind.

'Yes, speaking.'

'This is D C Peace of the West Yorkshire Police.'

'Oh, ye-e-es?'

'I believe you telephoned us earlier this evening about the refuge for the homeless in Portland Terrace.'

There was a long pause. Randolph Ingram pricked up his ears. This had all the hallmarks of one of Alicia's best-laid plans ganging agley, which they pretty oft did.

'I didn't give my name.'

It was an admission, without being an explicit admission. Alicia never had been good at owning up, preferring a genteel fudge.

'No, you didn't give your name. Will you answer my question, Mrs Ingram?'

'Well, yes, actually it was me. You see –'

'Right, can you tell me, Mrs Ingram, who was the source of the information you gave us that there were drugs behind the chest of drawers on the first-floor landing at 24 Portland Terrace?'

'Yes, I think I can tell you that,' said Alicia patronizingly, with a return of confidence. 'I'd had a phone call earlier from a young man – he sounded young – who refused to give his name.'

'Can you tell me anything about his voice? His accent for example?'

'Oh, just working-class Yorkshire, I'd say. His voice? Well, not very pleasant. Harsh almost. He was trying to be friendly, but . . .'

'But he didn't sound the friendly type. I see. Well, Mrs

84

Ingram, I'll need to ask you some questions about what happened earlier this evening at the refuge.'

'Oh? Why?'

'There's been an incident, a serious one. We'll call on you tomorrow.'

'Quite impossible, I'm afraid. I shall be away the next two or three days.'

'Mrs Ingram, this may well become a murder inquiry, and you witnessed, perhaps were involved in, a confrontation at the same address earlier in the evening. I would strongly advise you not to leave home until we have questioned you.'

'Well, we'll have to see about that, won't we?' said Alicia, in her softest, most condescending tone, and she put the phone down. 'Really, I don't know what the police are coming to. They've no respect any longer. And that was just a constable!'

'I expect it's all the white-collar crime they come in contact with,' said her husband, comfortably smiling to himself. He had long ago categorized his wife in his mind as ambitious, mendacious, and not very bright. He tried not to let her realize the pleasure he took in her discomfiture and aborted plots. And so far she never had.

Mike Oddie was seeing the two young people for the first time. The Chief Inspector had arrived at number twenty-four a few minutes before, had been given a rough outline of what had happened by Charlie, and had decided that the first thing to do was to get the details of the assault absolutely clear.

'Now, Ben Marchant and Midge – let's call her that, shall we? – had gone into the front room here to talk in private, is that right?' The two young heads nodded. 'What were they talking about?'

'The new situation, sir.' Mike's chief inspector status seemed to give him, in Alan's eyes, the sort of aura a senior schoolmaster would have. 'Whether the fact that both her father and Mr Siddiq said that they'd given up the idea of marriage for her really changed things.'

'Ben had talked to DC Peace about that earlier, I gather,' said Mike, looking round at Charlie, who nodded.

'We both agreed that caution was necessary.'

'I'm sure Midge would have gone along with that,' said Katy.

'Right. Now let's come to the attack. How long had Ben and Midge been talking?'

'About ten minutes maybe,' Alan said.

'No more than fifteen, anyway,' said Katy.

'And where were you both?'

'I was in here, watching *Soldier, Soldier,*' said Alan.

'And I was upstairs in my room reading.'

'So tell me exactly what happened – Alan first.'

Alan swallowed hard.

'There was this scream, then another. I thought for a moment it was on the television. They were in this deserted barracks, and I thought ... Anyway, it only took a second or two to realize it was coming through the wall, and then I was terrified. I got up, rushed through –'

'Hold on a bit. When you got to the hall, was it empty?'

'Yes.' Alan stopped, forehead furrowed. 'It was empty, but as I was opening the door to the back room here, I think I heard the front door shutting.'

'I think so too,' said Katy. 'I was on the landing, and you can't see the front door – the ceiling of the ground floor is very high, as you can see, and the stairs are steep – but I think I heard it shut.'

'Right. And you went into the front room, and – what?'

'And Midge was screaming in pain and holding her cheek, and Ben was in her lap, retching and bleeding from the throat and –' Alan put his face in his hands at the memory. 'It was the most horrible thing I've ever seen.'

Oddie let that subject go. They could probably get as much as they needed from Midge, eventually. He took them back over the day, taking in the phone call from Mrs Ingram, which Ben had told them about, the departure of Mouse, and then the visits of Mr Siddiq and Mrs Ingram.

'Could you see Mr Siddiq well?' Oddie asked Alan.

'Oh yes. Ben was on one side of the doorway, Zak and Pal on the other, and I was between them.'

'What was your impression of him?'

'I don't know . . . He seemed to be *trying* to be nice . . . I could see why Midge didn't like him – not just as a husband, I mean, but as a man.'

'Would you say that there was violence there, under the surface?'

Alan looked uncertain.

'No, I wouldn't want to say that. I wouldn't want to judge him like that . . . But there was something . . . A sort of frustration, I think.'

'Good – I see. Do you think it was frustration that he wasn't getting his own way?'

'Yes. I think he was used to getting it. Ben stopped him seeing Midge. But if all he wanted was to say the marriage was off, he didn't have to talk to her, did he?'

'No. And while this confrontation was going on, Mrs Ingram arrived, didn't she?'

'Yes. I didn't see her till she was at the gate. I didn't know who she was, because I'd never seen her before, but I guessed.'

'How?'

'Well, just because she looked very middle class, and was coming here. You wouldn't see many people dressed like that around here. And then because she seemed sort of pleased.'

'Pleased that there was a row going on?'

'Yes. Chuffed.'

'What did she actually do?'

Alan turned to Katy.

'I can't remember the exact words, can you?'

'I was way back. I could hardly hear.'

'It was something about having come at an inconvenient time. One of those phrases, said sort of snootily . . . And then there was something funny . . .'

'Yes?'

'She said she'd come back when things were more – and then she paused, and eventually said "normal". And I got this odd idea –' Oddie and Charlie waited, while he sorted his ideas out – 'this odd idea that she hadn't paused because she was searching for a word, like we all do, but because she was disconcerted for a moment by something she'd seen.'

'What could that be?'

Alan looked down, as if embarrassed, and afraid he was talking nonsense.

'Well, maybe some*one* she'd seen. Someone standing in the doorway, for example. It's just an idea.'

CHAPTER 10

Casualties

It was nearly eleven at night before they were able to talk to Midge. Constable Ryder, who had gone with her, phoned to say that she had been sewn up, was stable and quite calm and wanted to speak to them. They certainly wanted to talk to her. They left WPC Gould at the Centre, with three other uniformed policemen who had been drafted in, to get the preliminary questioning of the inmates of both houses properly under way.

At the hospital they were told that Ben Marchant was still in the operating theatre, so there was nothing to be done in that quarter. One of the locums they talked to shook his head.

'It's touch and go. He was only saved by being brought here so quickly. You won't be talking to him for a while. Better count on it being a long while.'

But when they had talked to Midge they wondered just how much Ben would be able to tell them.

Midge had been heavily bandaged over the stitches. The bits that they could see looked very beautiful, but very fragile too, and they wondered about the bits of her face they could not see, and whether the scars would be permanent. Talking was a little easier for her now, though far from pain-free. Charlie sat on her bed and Oddie on the chair beside it, and PC Ryder stood just outside the curtains of her cubicle, keeping an eye on all the comings and goings in a large hospital's accident and emergency unit.

'Is Ben all right?' Midge asked.

'He's still in the operating theatre,' Oddie replied. 'The doctor said it's pretty serious.'

Midge nodded, then winced.

'I knew. I knew when I was holding him that he might die. It's awful. He was doing so much good.'

'You'd been discussing whether you should go back to your family, hadn't you?'

'Yes.' Midge stopped herself nodding again. 'Not much to discuss, really. We agreed I should be cautious.'

'So you were going to stay at the Centre?'

'Yes. Ben had been doubtful about that before. I'm not really homeless in the usual sense, not in the sense the rest are, and once my father had found out where I was, Ben felt that it made sense for me to move on.'

'But he'd changed his mind?'

Midge's face, what they could see of it, assumed an expression that could only be described as inscrutable.

'I suppose so . . . I suppose my father saying he'd given up the marriage made it less urgent for me to move.'

'So Ben believed him?'

'Well, I don't know about that. He gave him the benefit of the doubt.'

'When we talked I emphasized the need to stay on your guard,' Charlie put in. 'He seemed to agree with that.'

'Oh, he did . . .' Midge hesitated, then seemed to make a decision. 'I think he'd got to like having me around. While we were talking he put his hand on mine – oh, not trying anything on, I don't mean that, but sort of fatherly. I think he felt affection for me is what I'm trying to say, though I don't want you to get the wrong impression. Definitely fatherly. I appreciated it, though I didn't want it to go too far. I have a father. Up till now I've loved him very much.'

'How were you sitting, when he was holding your hand?' Oddie asked.

'His hand was *on* mine – that's different,' Midge corrected him. 'I was sitting at the table nearest the door, looking towards the window. He'd pulled his chair out from the table, and was sitting looking straight at me.'

'With his back to the door too?'

'Yes. We were both at the same side of the table, with our backs to the door.'

'Had you seen anything through the window – anyone arrive at the house maybe?'

'No. I was too interested in what we were talking about.'

'Now, the attack, when it happened. How much did you see?'

Midge looked as if she would like to have screwed her face up, the memory of it paining her, but knew she mustn't.

'We were just sitting there talking quietly, unemotionally. The door was partly open – there was nothing secret about the talk. Then . . . it must have been opened further, someone must have come in . . .'

'Must have,' put in Charlie. 'You weren't conscious of it?'

'No. I saw no one, sensed no one, till – till I felt this terrible pain down my left cheek, and I just keeled over.'

'So you were attacked first?'

'Yes.'

'But if . . . *when* we talk to Ben Marchant, the likelihood is that he will have seen nothing either?'

Midge considered this.

'Maybe. I can't tell. Because there may have been a moment or two, between my getting slashed and him getting attacked, when he could have turned and caught a glimpse . . . But I was holding my head in my hands, not knowing what had happened to me, and I wasn't aware of what happened next. Not till I was holding him in my arms and –'

Mike Oddie held up his hand, and the two men got up. There was every reason not to distress her further that night. It must already have been the most traumatic day of her young life.

It was very late when they got back to Portland Terrace, but everyone was still up. WPC Gould had talked to most of them, or had had reports from the other uniformed constables, and she had prepared a little chart of who was where, at least notionally. Of course in a hostel such as this one they didn't stick to their rooms like prisoners in cells.

'Downstairs in number twenty-four, as you know, is the

91

kitchen, the dining room and the lounge with television – the communal area. Upstairs on the first floor there's a bedroom with Katy and Mehjabean in it, one with Zak, and one with Jezebel. I thought it would be easier if I used the names they're going under, sir.'

'Sure,' agreed Oddie. 'We may well have difficulty getting their real ones.'

'Then in the attic there's two bedrooms, one that had the boy they call Mouse in it –'

'I've seen that one,' Charlie said.

'Grateful little sod, wasn't he? And the other has a *very* young boy called Tony. I think we ought –'

Mike Oddie stopped her.

'Maybe. But first things first. What about number twenty-two?'

'Most of them are there, of course. The front room is split into two, and one has a boy called Simon in it, the other a girl called Rose – nicely spoken, but quiet.'

'Right. I've got that.'

'On the first floor upstairs Ben has one room, then there's a boy called Splat in one, and a girl called Bett Southcott in the other. Alan has one of the attic rooms, and a guy called Derek the other – probably the oldest here, I would guess.'

'They move in with each other now and then, I suppose?'

WPC Gould pursed her lips dubiously.

'A degree of that, but apparently not as much as you might expect. Ben, apparently, has always insisted on them having a room to themselves because they need their privacy after living communally on the streets. It seems that he is right. They value it.'

'Well, that's pretty clear. Thanks. We can't do much more that's serious tonight, but maybe we could talk to one or two. Makes sense to start with number twenty-four. We'll go up and chat to this Zak and his girlfriend. Tell all the others to go to bed. Tell them, if they're nervous, that there'll be a guard on the house – on both houses. We'll talk to them tomorrow.'

Then he looked at Charlie and the two of them went upstairs, Charlie leading the way to Zak's bedroom. Jezebel and Queenie were still there, but the two humans were sharing a companionable nightcap, while the two dogs were watching, waiting for night. Mike was getting a good look at them for the first time. Jezebel was wearing a long skirt, a black jumper with a hole in it over a T-shirt, and bright plastic beads. Zak had on dirty khaki trousers and a mud-smeared sports shirt: he had tattoos up one arm and a stud in his nose. His hair hadn't seen a comb in weeks, it seemed – in fact Pal was very much more kempt than his master, though not so spruce as to put off potential contributors to his welfare. Zak was very aware of Mike taking all this in.

'Me best clothes is in the wash,' he said. Mike grinned, and while Charlie sat on the floor, he took the one armchair.

'Any news of Ben?' Jezebel asked.

'Not good,' said Charlie. 'Touch and go. But they haven't given up hope.'

'That's diabolical,' said Zak. ''E were a great bloke.'

'Still is,' said Jezebel. 'Don't you bury him if the doctors haven't.'

'And what 'appens to this place if 'e dies?' Zak wanted to know.

Nobody knew the answer to that.

'How did you hear of it?' Mike asked, to stay on the subject.

''E cum round himself, talking to people on the streets. Gave out little bits o' paper wi' th'address on. Talked to us about ussel', and our lives and that.'

'Is that how you heard?' Mike asked Jezebel.

'No, that was word of mouth. There's this foul-mouthed old tart called Red Sal, sleeps up around the university science buildings. Claims to have once slept with the whole Bayern München football team of nineteen-whatever-it-was. Bet some of them took back a holiday souvenir they could have done without. Anyway, she was effing and blinding about people doing everything for the young homeless (I hadn't noticed) and nothing for the old ones. She'd got hold of one of those bits of paper with the address on it, and the words "Centre for the Homeless". I thought: "I'll try that."'

'Was that when the refuge first started?'

'Later,' said Zak. 'I bin 'ere from the start, but Jezebel, she cum later.'

'How did you both come to be on the streets?' Charlie asked. They treated it as the most normal question in the world.

'Me dad died when I were ten,' said Zak. 'Pit accident. I loved me dad. Then me mam took up wi' this bloke, and 'e were no good, an' before long 'e started knocking 'er about, an' I tried to 'elp, but she wouldn't let me – made up silly stories as to 'ow she'd got 'er cuts an' bruises. 'Fraid she were going to lose 'im, though that'd 'a been the best thing that could 'appen. Eventually I thought "Stuff this", and o' course there were no work in the mining villages, so it sempt the only thing I could do was to come to Leeds to look for a job. Didn't find one.'

Mike's eyes shifted to Jezebel.

'Fancied getting away from home. Wanted my freedom. Mum's OK, but she had all these rules and regulations at home, and they riled me. So I just took off. I knew I could survive – not like some. I give her a bell now and then, and I suppose some day I'll go back. It's no big deal.'

No big deal – except that she had probably incapacitated herself for work, for any kind of settled life.

'Has the hostel made a difference?' he asked her.

Jezebel was positively enthusiastic.

'It's great! It's like having a bedsitter, without having to pay rent, and without any obligations or sweat. I think Ben's done a great job – and those kids are good too.'

'There's several as 've found jobs from 'ere,' said Zak, 'settled down. Not that 'e puts pressure on anyone to do that, but if that's what you want, 'aving this place is a big 'elp.'

'Is that what you want?' Charlie asked him. Zak waited a moment, then shrugged.

'I've applied for one or two this past month. No go. Don't know what I'd do about Pal if I got one.'

He looked at the dog, who beat his stringy, whiplash tail on the floor, conscious of attention.

'There's any of us would take him during the day,' said Jezebel.

'Pal's me best mate. I don't know as I'd give 'im to anyone else, even for the daytime.'

Charlie thought he was half wanting to get a job, half fearful of the changes he would have to make to his life – and maybe feeling in his heart he could never fit into normal society again. All these seemed perfectly normal reactions, in the circumstances.

'Let's go through what happened today,' Mike Oddie said.

Alternating and contradicting each other, they went through the various happenings, some of which they had seen, others they had heard about. Rumour went through the Centre not with the hectic, involved urgency of rumours in an English village, but with the fatalistic retelling appropriate to people who have contracted out of the usual social concerns and relationships, and in whose lives anything may happen. If the Centre were under threat, if it had to close, they would be sadder and poorer and hungrier, but life would go on. Knocks were what they were most used to. Oddie questioned Zak closely about the confrontation on the front doorstep.

'You could see Mr Siddiq, and Mrs Ingram as well?'

'Course I could. Siddiq were real close. 'E weren't the sort of bloke for a cracker like Midge.'

'Why not?'

'Too bleedin' old, wannee? Not very nice, either. Wouldn't take 'im at 'is word, that's for sure.'

'And Mrs Ingram you couldn't see quite so well, I suppose?'

'Well enough. Snooty old git, and pushy with it. Pleased as Punch there was a bit of a barney going on.'

'Have you talked over with Alan what happened while she was standing at the gate?' Charlie asked.

'Standing at the gate? Nothing much 'appened while she were standing at the gate.'

'What she said, then.'

'No. Should I 'ave?'

'No, it's a good thing you didn't. Could we have your account of it?'

'Well . . . I don't know. Like I say, nothing much 'appened.' Zak looked at Jezebel, uncertain.

'I was back in the hall. I didn't see anything much, though I could hear her.'

Zak pondered.

'She sailed up, stood at the gate, saw what was going on, then said one of those phrases they use' (he could have been talking about a lost tribe of savages) 'you know, something about 'aving come at the wrong time.'

'Yes,' said Charlie encouragingly.

'Then she said she'd come back when . . . what was it? . . . when things were back to normal.'

'Can you remember how she said it?'

This flummoxed Zak, and he struggled with his memories.

'Didn't she pause before she said "normal", like she was trying to find the right word?' asked Jezebel. 'Or maybe the most insulting word.'

'She *stopped*', said Zak, 'before she said the word "normal". But I don't know if she were trying to find the right word. It were more as if . . .' he screwed up his face, and the ring in his nose jiggled, 'as if she'd been stopped in 'er tracks . . . surprised, like.'

Charlie would have preferred to wait until he became more specific, but with Zak you could have waited for ever.

'What could she have been surprised at?' he asked. Zak shrugged.

'Search me. One of us, I suppose. But it weren't me. I don't mix wi' toffs like 'er, an' I never 'ave done. So it must 'ave been Ben or Alan.'

Five minutes later, as they got into their car, Mike Oddie said to Charlie, 'Confirmation! Alan is an observant lad. What's the odds she recognized Ben Marchant?'

'I'd say it was pretty certain. But it's odd she hadn't recognized his voice on the phone.'

'Or hadn't let on that she had.'

'If she had, she wouldn't have been surprised when she saw him,' Charlie pointed out.

'True. It's late. I'm not thinking straight. But I do know that we're going to have to face up to the fact that Ben Marchant had a life of – what? – forty years or more before he ever set up the refuge here in Portland Terrace.'

Charlie nodded.

'And maybe Mrs Ingram is the one to tell us something about it. I think we should go and see her first thing tomorrow.'

But when they called on her, they found that the bird had flown.

CHAPTER 11

Bosom of the Family

'My wife? Oh, I'm afraid you've missed her. She made an early start to go on a surprise visit to her mother.'

Randolph Ingram was of medium height, but seemed taller by reason of his distinguished appearance – broad, courtly, but with an ironic smile that played on his lips even when giving out such mundane information. They had noticed when they flashed their identification at him that there was a contrast between his respectable exterior – he was a bursar at Leeds' second university, they had discovered in advance – and the relishing sparkle in his eyes. Then again, Charlie thought, perhaps the information he had just given them was not entirely mundane: possibly he had taken care to insert the fact that the visit Alicia was paying to her mother was a 'surprise' one.

'Mr Ingram,' Oddie began, 'your wife was warned –'

He shrugged this aside, still imperturbably urbane.

'Oh, Alicia takes very badly to warnings and prohibitions. They seem to act as challenges. There was a time when I could always get her to do what I wanted by telling her to do the opposite. It was the same with Emily Brontë, I'm told. Unfortunately Alicia has at least got wise to that one over the years.'

'It's a serious matter, Mr Ingram, to disobey police orders in this way.'

'Well, that's something you'd best take up with Alicia. She is her own mistress, as I expect you will have guessed.'

'What precisely is her interest in the refuge for the homeless at Portland Terrace, Mr Ingram?' Charlie asked.

Randolph Ingram stood relaxed and elegant against his own doorpost.

'Ah well, it's an issue, you see. Alicia's very political at the moment – she's going all out to get the Conservative nomination for the Bramsey ward. The refuge is an issue, something she can work up indignation about in the party.'

'I see . . . There's nothing personal in it?'

He shrugged.

'Personal? Not as far as I'm aware. Things aren't going well for the Tories at the moment. If she doesn't have an issue it's very unlikely the seat will stay Conservative. The buzz at the moment in local Conservative circles is that Alicia will get the nomination, which does surprise me a little.'

'Oh?'

'The last thing most people want at the moment is a BMW.'

'I beg your pardon?'

'BMW. Bossy middle-class woman. Hardly the flavour of the post-Thatcher decade. Look how people react to Virginia Bottomley. My guess is that they want to give her the nomination, let her lose the seat, and that will put paid to her political aspirations for good.'

'Very Machiavellian,' Oddie commented.

'All politicians are, even at the grass-roots level.'

'You know your wife went to the Centre last night?'

'Did she? No, she didn't actually tell me. Though I knew something was up.'

'Oh? How?'

'I know my wife. And she made this sudden decision to visit her mother and sister, though she's largely washed her hands of them in recent years.'

'I see. And you've no idea of any connection between your wife and anyone at the Centre?'

'None whatsoever. It seems unlikely. Alicia usually only cultivates people who matter.'

'Could you tell me the address of your wife's mother and sister?'

'Of course. Clematis Cottage, Hartridge, Lincolnshire. It's a tiny village, and you can't miss the cottage if you recognize clematis. In that, as in many other respects, Alicia's mother has overdone things.'

When the policemen had said their thanks and farewells, Randolph Ingram closed the door and went to collect together his papers and briefcase for work, the ironic smile playing more openly on his lips. The policemen must have thought him remarkably loose-tongued – though really there must be many people who would enjoy being similarly honest about their wives or husbands. Alicia had been his main source of amusement for years. He had come to the conclusion some time ago that, if she should die, he would miss her but not regret her. The same would be true if she were to disappear for a long prison sentence.

But that wasn't really on the cards, was it? Ruthless as Alicia was in going for what she wanted, Randolph could not see his wife as a murderess. Though in recent months he had begun to see her as someone he had had enough of, the possibility of being shot of her in *that* way was not one he had ever considered.

Yet she *was* ruthless, she was entirely without principle . . .

In the car, on the way back to police headquarters at Millgarth, Oddie said: 'He wasn't holding much back, was he?'

'Dobbing her right in,' said Charlie, nodding. 'And pleased with himself for doing it.'

'I suppose the *why* doesn't concern us. The state of the Ingram marriage can't have anything to do with the case. The question is, what do we do about his wife?'

'Going just by the voice, she has a talking-down-to-dim-five-year-olds quality that riles me,' said Charlie.

'But of course we couldn't possibly accept your being riled as a reason for acting nasty, could we? On the other hand, I don't like people who are warned to be available for questioning, then deliberately take off. And this was *not* a long-planned family visit, you notice.'

'As her husband took care to point out,' Charlie said.

'Why has she gone down to visit her long-neglected

mother and sister, when presumably she has plenty of other friends or contacts around the country she could go off visiting?' asked Oddie.

'Because of something that happened at the Centre last night?' suggested Charlie. He thought for a bit, and then said: 'Lincolnshire isn't the end of the earth.'

It was plain sailing to decide that Charlie should go: Mike Oddie had no liking for long car journeys, whether on business or pleasure. He was also itching to get down to talking to the young people at the refuge.

'Including Alan Coughlan and Katy Bourne,' he said. 'You've never found out how he made contact with them, have you?'

'No – except I think it must have been out of the blue.'

'Pretty devastating at that age, psychologically speaking, finding you have a father you didn't know about. And in Alan's case a father who replaces a father he did know about. We have to remember that both of them were in number twenty-four at the time of the attack. They're very much in the frame.'

Charlie accepted this judgement, though he didn't much like it. His trip down to Hartridge was uneventful, and its freedom from the usual motorway irritations and delays meant that he could think through his approach in the forthcoming encounter. He wished he had thought to press Randolph Ingram on whether his wife had announced her intention to visit her mother before he had phoned to tell her he would want to question her. His own impression was that the home visit was not instantaneously improvised but was an existing intention – though certainly not an unchangeable intention that ruled out an interview with him. Was it, then, a decision made *after* the visit to the refuge and *before* his phone call? If so, it seemed almost inevitable that the decision was connected with her visit to the refuge.

Hartridge was indeed a tiny village of about fifteen houses, one of them a converted pub. No pub, no shop, no bus service as far as Charlie could see. Rural life could only be sustained there these days by constant recourse to the motor car.

Clematis Cottage was indeed obvious. Charlie wasn't hot on botanical niceties, but he trained sometimes in Golden Acre Park, where there was an avenue of various strains of clematis – mostly dead, but enough living to tell him what they looked like. The front and sides of one of the cottages was ablaze with pink, puce and purple flowers, with a particularly large and threatening mauve-and-white striped variety which seemed to stare the visitor in the face and dare him to call it ugly.

There was a small garage beside the cottage, with an old car inside it and another car, a brick-coloured Volvo, in the drive leading to it. Charlie drew his own car up in the road outside the front door, and left the windows open. The front garden of the cottage was a mere handkerchief, and the windows of the cottage were open. He heard quite distinctly an old woman's voice – raised because she was going deaf and thought everybody else was. The tone was determined rather than querulous – a strong, individual voice.

'No, Alicia, no, no, no. You come down here once in a blue moon, and when you do you want to boss us all around, tell us how to run our lives, and stick your finger in every pie going. You can't even make up your mind what you want. Last night it was one thing, today it's another –'

Charlie heard Mrs Ingram's voice breaking in, but though it was by now familiar – a note or two too high for comfort, with its maddeningly precise articulation – the only word he could distinguish was 'misunderstanding'.

'Alicia, I may be nearly blind and slightly deaf, but I am not a fool, and I won't be talked to as if I were one. I understood perfectly what you said on the phone last night. Carol and I talked it over – not that we needed to – and –'

But she was interrupted by a cry, a shriek, something that sounded somewhere between a human in pain and a sardonic tropical bird. Charlie closed his window and, as the cry was repeated, sped through the gate and up to the front door.

The ring silenced the weird, unearthly sound. There was total silence for a few seconds inside. It was Alicia who opened the door. Charlie recognized the voice, even from her 'Yes?'

'Mrs Ingram? D C Peace, of the Leeds police.'

She barely looked at his ID but stared at him with an outraged expression on her face.

'You're a policeman?'

It was not said with incredulity, but with distaste.

'Yes, that's right. I spoke to you last night, and warned you we had to talk to you.'

'This is too ridiculous! You expect me to disrupt my carefully arranged schedule for a silly matter like a fracas at a hostel for the homeless. I told you last night I had no intention of doing so. Trouble among people like that must be a daily occurrence.'

'Mrs Ingram, if you do not allow me to interview you for as long as I think necessary, I am authorized to arrest you and take you back to Leeds. I don't think that would do your political prospects any good, do you? Now, may I come in?'

Alicia thought, none too quickly, then grudgingly stood aside.

A door from the tiny hallway led into the main room of the cottage. Three people were sitting there: an old woman with brown wrinkled skin and wild grey hair, peering with avid curiosity in his direction; a heavy, younger woman, her face already lined with worry; and in a wheelchair a fair-haired boy of about twelve, his head permanently twisted sideways and upwards, his mouth open. As Charlie entered he uttered another of those cries.

'Who is it, Alicia?'

'A policeman, Mother. It's just a little matter he wants a word with me about.'

'A policeman from Spalding, or a policeman from Leeds?'

'I'm from Leeds, Mrs –' said Charlie.

'Mrs Boulting. And these are Carol and Jeremy. From Leeds? Then it can hardly be a little matter, can it? Why can't you be a better liar, Alicia? Practice doesn't make even moderately competent in your case . . . You're black, aren't you, Mr Policeman?'

'D C Peace. That's right, I'm black.'

'Ahhh! How exciting we used to find black men in my young days!'

'Mother!'

'Oh, but we did, Alicia. There was that jazz trumpeter at the Savoy, Jerry "Hot" Sylvester. Sheer bliss in *every* way! Then the black servicemen here in Lincolnshire, over from America for the duration of the war. Absolute darlings. Do women still find black men exciting, Mr Peace?'

'Some do, Mrs Boulting. Some definitely do.'

'I'm so glad. It's always good to find some things that don't change.' The unearthly cry came again from the direction of the wheelchair. Charlie felt that discomfiting mixture of compassion and unease that many feel in the presence of mental sickness. Alicia's sister went over and put her hands comfortingly on the boy's shoulders. The boy relaxed at once. 'Is it time for his walk in the garden?' the old woman asked.

'More than time,' said her daughter. She looked at her sister reproachfully. 'He's been upset by all the aggravation.'

'Carol, if you would only see sense –'

'Well, Alicia,' said their mother, struggling to her feet and aiming herself by sense rather than sight for the kitchen and the back door, 'we'll leave you to your chat with the nice policeman. We'd love to stay and hear what you've been doing, but I don't suppose that we'd be welcome. Come along, Jeremy: it's time for your turn around the garden.'

Oddie looked at the girl on the other side of the table. She was not particularly dirty, not dressed or decorated in the insignia of the homeless. And she was not particularly *there* at all. He could feel P C Gould – a no-nonsense woman – stir in her seat beside him in irritation. Rose seemed to be on cloud nine, and occasionally sent down monosyllabic messages therefrom. If she was not on drugs – and he assumed that Ben Marchant had investigated such an obvious possibility – then he wondered what it was afflicting her.

'You're in the front room of next door, number twenty-two, aren't you?'

A pause, while the query seemed to be received, stored,

then analysed for content. Eventually an answer was transmitted.

'Yes.'

'Have you been coming to the refuge for long?'

Each question resulted in that same pause, the same dreamy analysis.

'About two months.'

'Where do you sleep when you're not here?'

'Near the parish church.'

'How long have you been sleeping rough?'

This was a really difficult one, requiring a long session of consideration.

'I don't know . . . months . . . a year . . .'

'Where was your home before that?'

'Chester . . . near Chester.'

'Are your parents still there?'

'My father is.'

'Won't he be worried about you? Shouldn't you contact him, maybe think of going back to live with him?'

Something like acute pain went across her face.

'Not after what he did . . . not after that . . . And the police believed him, not me . . . I'll never see him again.'

When they questioned her about the events of the previous night she just shook her head. She had noticed nothing, heard nothing. Oddie had expected this. She lived apart, shut off, enclosed. She needed psychiatric help. So did many, maybe most, of those sleeping rough. How did you ensure that they got it, even supposing there was anybody interested enough to try and give them what they needed?

'Well, let's get it over with,' said Alicia crossly. She was unable to disguise it when she got cross. She sat down briskly and looked up at him. 'It seems a great waste, coming all this way on such a trivial matter.'

'Marchant may well die,' said Charlie brutally, but her face showed no reaction. 'I'm sure you don't normally treat murder as something roughly on a par with illegal parking.'

There was still no shadow of concern. He sat down, and for the first time took in the room: shabby, much-used furniture, reproductions of favourite paintings on the walls, photographs everywhere, including some very old ones – from the thirties he guessed – of an extremely elegant lady who was also a decidedly sexy one. If he looked out into the garden he had no doubt he would see the lady herself.

'What is your interest in Ben Marchant's refuge for the homeless?' he asked. Alicia pursed her tight little mouth.

'The interest of any concerned citizen,' she said. 'Bramsey is not at all the right place for something like that.'

'I see. But not everyone would be so active, when it's not actually anywhere near your own home.'

'Any *concerned* person would –' She pulled herself up. 'Oh well, I suppose you know: I have a political interest in Bramsey. I'm hoping to be Conservative candidate for the ward on Leeds City Council. So people have started bringing all their worries about the area to me.'

'I see. What sort of people are these?'

'The old couple in the house opposite, for example.'

'Anybody else? Has Mr Haldalwa been to see you?'

'Well, yes . . . Yes, actually he has.'

'So you've taken an interest in his daughter and her marriage?'

She shook her head vigorously, mouth pursed still tighter.

'Not specifically. Naturally the last thing I would do is interfere in a personal, private matter. But of course that does show the sort of trouble that can arise if you collect together undesirables in the way Mr Marchant has been doing.'

'Right . . . So last night you went round there.'

'Yes. And of course there was trouble.'

'Trouble? I understood the situation as being that the proposed bridegroom was there to give the news that he was withdrawing from the proposed marriage.'

'You weren't there,' said Alicia dogmatically. 'The whole refuge was at the two front doors, ganging up on this man – a very ugly situation.'

'So you withdrew?'

'It seemed best. I could hardly do anything useful in the circumstances.'

'But not before you recognized Mr Marchant.'

She didn't bat an eyelid, or pause.

'That's right.'

'You didn't recognize his voice on the phone, but you did in fact know him.'

'Know him? I wouldn't exactly say that. I knew who he was. I don't suppose I'd ever heard his voice. He used to be estate manager for Sir George Mallaby.'

'I don't think I know the name.'

She looked scornful.

'You ought to. He's big locally. Has a big house and farm out past Otley. Basically he's a businessman, self-made, and he always has a manager running the estate. Wife's a bit of a snob, with no good reason.'

Charlie felt like asking her to go through the good reasons for being a snob. Instead he said:

'And you met Ben Marchant there?'

'Saw him. I was out there – now what was it about? Oh yes, it was a committee meeting of the Leeds Piano Competition Committee. Lady Mallaby had muscled in there, of course. And as we were all leaving, he and Sir George were talking in the reception hall of Belstone Manor.'

Charlie wondered about this story, but he remained inscrutable.

'You have a remarkable memory for faces.'

'I've always had at the back of my mind the thought that I might go in for politics – maybe in a small way at first. In politics a good memory is a *sine qua non*.'

'So when you recognized –'

But they were interrupted by a cry from the garden, then by another and another. Alicia responded as if on autocue.

'Oh, that poor wretch. He's having one of his really bad turns. Carol has no idea how to deal with him at all. Do excuse me –'

And she rushed out, unable to let anything of moment happen that she didn't play a principal role in. Charlie was glad. It gave him a chance to examine the photographs around the room. In particular it allowed him to examine one he had earlier noticed which had been turned face down on the dark, chipped old sideboard. It could be chance or accident that it had been turned down, of course. But when he took it up and looked at it, he very much doubted if it was.

Because it showed – younger, more carefree, her face in particular much less lined – the unmistakable figures of Ben Marchant and Alicia's sister Carol.

CHAPTER 12

Sisters

Charlie's reactions thereafter were based on instinct rather than on normal police procedures. That is to say they were based on experience, judgement of character, assessment of situation, and flair. As uproar in the garden continued – not just the distressing cries of the boy Jeremy, but loud hostility between sister and sister – he replaced the photograph as he had found it, let himself silently out of the front door, slipped round and noted the number of the brick-coloured Volvo, then got into his car and drove away in the direction of Leeds.

There was a suitable pub, the George Washington, just before he got to the A15: it had parking out the back, was built directly on the road, and looked as if it served a good pint. Charlie ordered a half from a pot-bellied, genial landlord, immediately corrected that to a pint, then took up his position at the window. It was mid morning, and he was the only customer. The landlord was intrigued.

'Watching for someone?' he asked.

'Someone in a car. I'm a policeman, by the way. Want to see my ID?'

'No, mate. It's all one to me. But if it's going to be a shoot-out, warn me, because we're not used to that kind of thing down this neck of the woods.'

'No shoot-out, I promise. I'm just backing a hunch. Lovely pint this. I hope I don't get interrupted . . . Know anything about the Boultings in Hartridge?'

'Mother and daughter? They come in here now and then, mostly lunchtimes. Not big spenders, but pleasant. Mother's been a goer in her time, but she's a real character. Sad about the young lad. They're devoted to him, both of them. I hope they're not in any trouble?'

'Not so far as I know. They're just part of a jigsaw. Know who the father of the boy was?'

'No idea. He was a toddler when they moved here. Village life these days, it's all incomers. You wouldn't find a farm worker who could afford a cottage in Hartridge, yet the people who move there are not rich by any means. I've heard say the Boultings lived in Lincoln before they moved here, so they're not outright foreigners by our lights.'

Charlie stood there in companionable silence with the landlord for some twenty minutes or so. It needed no particular vigilance to recognize the car when it came. The brick-coloured Volvo could be seen driven peremptorily along the road from Hartridge, and, as it passed the George Washington, Charlie could spot Alicia by her hair alone, even though the driver's side was furthest from him. He turned back to the bar, carrying the last half of his pint. He grinned at the host.

'No particular point in hurrying, I suppose,' he said. 'The two ladies probably aren't going anywhere.'

'They're nice people, even if the mother is a bit over the top,' he said. 'Go easy on them.'

'Do I look like the sort of person who beats up old ladies and spastic kids?'

'Hmm. You look as if you could take care of yourself.'

'That's another matter. I did used to manage a gym,' Charlie conceded. 'Though as I remember most of the customers were a right collection of cissies and show-offs.'

He finished his pint and drove back in the direction of the village of Hartridge. This time the person who opened the door was Carol Boulting.

'Oh, it's you,' she said, but not unwelcomingly. 'I'm afraid Alicia's gone.'

Charlie decided to come clean.

'I know she has. I saw her driving towards Leeds.'

'And you came back to talk to us?' A grin lit up her heavy, lined face. 'Well, do come in. But if it's dirt on Alicia you're

110

after, I'm afraid you've come to the wrong people. We know very little about Alicia's activities in Leeds. She only comes here once in a blue moon, when her compulsive itch to interfere has nothing better to exercise itself on up there.' She led the way through to the living room. 'Jeremy's fine now. He reacts badly to any kind of disturbance or quarrel, so could we keep it nice and calm?'

'Of course. No reason why it should be anything else.'

'Mother, it's Mr Peace again. The policeman.'

Mrs Boulting, sprawled limply in an armchair, perked up at once.

'Oh, how *delicious*. You know where you're appreciated. But I'm afraid we're not at all *au fait* with what Alicia gets up to, if that's what you want to talk about. It's not men in her case, but power, you know. She always was an assertive kind of child. The head-girl type. My husband insisted the girls went to "good" schools, but in Alicia's case they seem to have taught her nothing but snobbery and aggression. Why I took my husband's advice on that I can't think. I didn't take it on anything else. We were separated by then, of course, and I suppose I thought that if he was willing to pay the bills, it would get her out of my hair.'

Charlie sat down on the other side of the hearth, while Carol remained standing, watching Jeremy.

'What I'm actually interested in is your daughter's connection with a man who runs a refuge for homeless young people in Leeds.'

The near-blind eyes almost sparkled up at him.

'That wouldn't be Ben Marchant by any chance, would it?'

'Yes. He was attacked last night and very badly hurt.'

'Poor Ben!' said Carol. 'He's so kind and generous. People take advantage.'

'This is worse than taking advantage,' Charlie said. He was intrigued. There was no sense of bitterness or hatred in Carol's voice. Yet Ben was presumably a former boyfriend – at the very least. 'I saw the photograph,' he said, gesturing to the frame.

'Oh!' said Mrs Boulting, peering at it, 'someone's turned it on its face.'

'I could guess who did that,' said Charlie. 'Could you tell me how well you know or knew Ben Marchant?'

'Knew,' said Carol. 'He's Jeremy's father. We haven't seen him in years.'

'When did you know him well?'

'Jeremy's eleven, so that gives you the rough idea.' She sat down, still casting regular glances at her son. 'We were living – Mother and I – just outside Lincoln then. I had a job – in a dress shop, can you believe it? Ben was at the Agricultural College nearby. He was a pretty mature student, but quite a lot of them were, so he wasn't out of place. We had a bit of a fling and –'

She gestured towards the wheelchair.

'Was there never any question of your getting married?'

'Oh no. He had always said "I'm not the marrying type", but he didn't even need to say it. I knew that.'

'And accepted it?'

'Yes, completely.'

'And you don't feel bitter now?'

'*No.*' She turned and directed at him an unswerving, challenging look. 'What you mean is, because my son turned out to have cerebral palsy, I should feel bitter because he gives me so much work. Well, you've got it entirely wrong. I love my son, my life centres round him. It's a lot better than having it centred on a dress shop, when you come to think about it, isn't it?'

'I suppose so. I'm sorry if I offended you. What happened when the relationship ended?'

'It ended when his course finished at college. He got a job in Derbyshire and took off. I'd always known he would. I wasn't the only girlfriend he had in this area, by the way.'

'By then Jeremy was born?'

'Oh yes – he was about one. In case you're interested, we did talk about having an abortion and I wasn't interested. When I knew there might be . . . medical problems, I still wasn't interested. So please don't see me as a victim, and please don't start imagining any resentment on my part

112

towards Ben. I loved him briefly, I liked him as long as he was around, and I'm sure I would still like him if I still knew him. I shall go and pray for his recovery at Evensong tonight.'

Charlie nodded, accepting.

'I'd still like to know where you both were last night.'

'Here. We're always here. Mrs Marsh next door popped in to watch *Coronation Street* and *The Bill* because her television's on the blink. Does that give us an alibi?'

'Yes, it should do. I wasn't very keen on the idea of a ten-year period of gestation for murder. Now – about your sister.'

The young man called Splat was a type that Oddie had had dealings with often enough before, but one that still made him feel strangely uneasy. Tattoos he'd been used to all his life, though Splat's seemed unusually flamboyant and all-covering (where did he get the money for artwork of this complexity?), but rings on nose, ears and lips (wasn't that horribly uncomfortable?) he still found repellent, as he did the brilliantly fluorescent colouring of the hair. It wasn't just that Splat made him feel middle-aged, conventional, horribly safe and middle-of-the-road. It was that he seemed to represent some kind of challenge, and Oddie couldn't quite put his finger on what, in himself, was being challenged.

He could almost have predicted Splat's history, however.

'I was in homes,' Spat said. 'I never knew me dad, and when I was six me mam just took off wi' a bloke, so they told me. Don't remember her, to tell you the truth – she's just a voice, shouting at me, now. So I was in homes after that. Couple o' times they got me a foster home, but it didn't work out, and I went back to a home.'

'Why didn't it work out?'

'I expect it was my fault. I wasn't used to families – didn't know what they were all about. I preferred what I knew. I could be king o' the castle in a home, because I knew how they worked. In a family I was expected to co-operate with the others, and I didn't know how to. Still don't.'

'How did you land up on the streets?'

'Easy. Just took off, didn't I? They were getting ready to chuck me out, so I did it for them.'

'How long ago was that?'

That bothered Splat. Time was something he had contracted out of.

'Six or seven years. Don't know exactly.'

'How do you survive?'

A shifty look came into his eyes.

'Beg an' that.'

He was grateful to Ben for providing the refuge, but he had no pipe dreams about getting a job or settling down and becoming part of the community. He thought he'd probably be dead by thirty ('an' that's all right by me'). He had heard nothing the previous night until all at number twenty-two had gone down to witness the confrontation on the doorstep of number twenty-four. He'd heard nothing after that, though he agreed he could have gone next door, even if the door had been locked, because he had a key. They all had, while they were in residence.

'We all could have done it, but none of us would. Ben is a good bloke. We all appreciate what he's done.'

'The chap called Mouse doesn't seem to have been grateful.'

'Oh, Mouse – he's a basket case,' said Splat, putting a great distance between himself and Mouse.

'So did your sister know Ben Marchant when you and he were going together?'

'Alicia? No, they never met. Alicia was married to Joe Newsome then – the father of Paul and Susannah – though she may have been starting the affair with Randolph. Joe was eminently acceptable socially, but extremely unsatisfactory as a husband and father.'

Mrs Boulting then took over the answering. She felt strongly on the subject of her elder daughter.

'Alicia has very little to do with us, as you probably gathered earlier. But periodically she *descends* on us when the meddling itch has nothing better to feed on, and organizes our lives for us. If it's small matters, we just say "Yes, Alicia" and wait for her to go away – which she does in almost indecent haste, feeling a great glow that she has "put things right".'

'But if it's an important matter?'

'If it's an important matter, like putting Jeremy into a home, of course we have to fight.'

'Why should she want Jeremy put into a home?'

Mrs Boulting looked at her daughter. Charlie had a sense of great closeness between the once-beauty and this plain, middle-aged woman.

'We've discussed this, haven't we, Carol? Alicia doesn't like being associated with anything ugly, or anything disturbing. I'm afraid she sees Jeremy as both. She's always talking about having things done with *style*. It's difficult to have style when you don't have full control of yourself, isn't it? And since she's always trying to bully other people into thinking as she does – she has no sense of other people being different, no sense of the beauty of variety and diversity – she periodically comes down here to tell us how much fuller and richer our lives would be if we put Jeremy into care somewhere.'

'Instead of which they would be infinitely emptier and poorer,' said Carol.

'Of course when that happens we have a row,' said Mrs Boulting. She clapped her hands. 'I love a row. Carol is no good at rowing, and hates having one because it disturbs Jeremy. That leaves a great gap in my life. I fill it up with the church – infinite scope for rows there, thank God, and the only reason I go, because I'm not at all sure that I *believe* in any meaningful way. Then there's the occasional visit from Alicia to satisfy my war-lust. By now you will have guessed that I thoroughly dislike Alicia.'

'How did you come to grow so far apart?'

'It happened, as I've said, when she went away to boarding school. Every holiday we seemed more and more to be strangers to each other . . . But, I don't know, maybe it was in the make-up, in the genes. My husband's mother was just the same – a Labour politician who loved organizing people for their own good. It was to have a more disorderly life than

115

that that George married me. And really we did have fun for a while. Parties and drugs and sleeping around – just like young people today. I suppose Alicia is reverting to type by going into politics, even if it is with a different party. And of course it's the Tories who are the bossy, preachy party now.'

'The question is, why did Mrs Ingram decide to descend on you today?' said Charlie.

'Right,' said Mrs Boulting determinedly. 'And I suspect that on that *you* may have to enlighten *us*.'

Sexual intercourse, Philip Larkin believed, began in 1963. It was around that time, in Oddie's mind, that the British lost the art of bringing up children. Bett Southcott was a malevolent, whingeing example of that process in the late stage.

'No, I don't *have* to be on the bleeding streets,' she said, looking from one to the other of her interrogators with no sense that she was making a bad impression. 'Or in this bleeding hostel, come to that. It's my cow of a mother. Can't stand the idea of me ever having a good time.'

'I shouldn't have thought sleeping rough represented any sort of good time,' said Oddie. Once again he had felt W P C Gould stir in irritation on the chair beside him in the dining room of number twenty-four.

"Course it doesn't. It's bleeding rough, and its scary. But I'll show her. Rules, rules, rules, that's all I ever had from her. Well, she'll come round and I'll go back on my terms. She's set my gran against me, otherwise I'd have gone to live with her yonks ago.'

'So will you tell me what happened last night?'

'Oh God, last night! They call this place a *refuge*, and you get the same sort of hassle as you get on the streets.'

The events of the day before seemed to have revived in her all the resentment and sense of grievance that had made Katy for one her enemy from the beginning of her time at the hostel. It was obvious she was on the streets not because she couldn't help it, but for a purpose of her own. Either she would achieve it, or she would go back to the genteel comfort of her mother's house on her mother's terms. In the meanwhile she did have one piece of useful information. Her account of the confrontation added nothing to what they knew, and was marked by her total lack of interest in anyone other than herself. It was for the period after that that she was able to shed a new ray of light.

'I came in here ten minutes before it happened,' she said. 'It could have been me that was attacked. I wanted to make some coffee – we've got gas rings in our rooms, but I'd run out of milk. I came to see if there was any in the fridge. Of course there wasn't a bleeding drop. I complained to Alan, who was slumped in front of the television.'

'Did you hear anything from this room?'

''Course I did. The door was open. Ben and that Paki girl were talking. Anyway, the front door was locked when I came in, and I locked it again when I went out. So unless someone else came in before it happened and left it unlocked, whoever did it had a key.'

'The thing is,' said Mrs Boulting, 'she rang last night – oh, about half past nine it would be. Said she'd discovered where Jeremy's father was. You'd have thought we'd been employing her as a private eye.'

'In fact, we'd never tried to find him,' said Carol, 'and had never even told Alicia his name.'

'Nor had she ever expressed much interest in "finding" him before,' said her mother, 'beyond a general expression of the view that he ought to help with the special expenses Jeremy's condition creates. All she knew about him was that photograph, and we took care not to let the name slip.'

'Why?'

'Because of her insatiable need to interfere. Jeremy is Carol's business, our business. It was our way of saying Keep Out, not letting her know his name. Then suddenly there she is on the phone saying she knows where he is, that Carol should sue him for maintenance, make him contribute to a nursing home for Jeremy.'

'What did you do?'

'Told her to mind her own business, as usual. But she said that from what she'd heard he had had a big lottery win and kept on and on about him paying a hefty whack for his past sins and for avoiding his responsibilities up to now.'

'What did you say to that?'

'Carol took over the call, said "Bully for Ben", and refused to consider suing him. After a minute or two she simply put the phone down.'

'But not before she'd threatened a visit today,' said Carol. 'That was why I put the phone down.'

'Right,' said Charlie, meditating. 'But, as I understand it, when she arrived today she had changed her tune?'

'Definitely. Though she couldn't do a 180-degree turn, because even she could see she would never convince us we had misheard or misunderstood to that extent. But she did her best. Now the talk was all about making cautious contact, telling him about Jeremy, congratulating him on his good fortune, suggesting we meet to discuss his future, and so on. No talk about suing, none of this "he ought to be exposed" rant.'

'Yesterday she was *News of the World*, today she was Marjorie Proops,' said Mrs Boulting. 'Of course she was up to something, both times. But what had happened to change her tune?'

'The matter I came to see her about,' said Charlie. 'The attempted murder. If it's not by now murder itself.'

The women's eyes were avid with interest. If he went back to Leeds and arrested Alicia they'd probably go for a celebratory drink at the George Washington that evening. Families – Charlie would never understand them.

CHAPTER 13

Refugees

The very large young man (only he did not give off the feel of being young) sat slumped in his chair on the other side of the dining table and told Oddie that his name was Simon Prentice. It was the first time Oddie had been favoured with a surname by any of the male residents in the refuge. He conjectured that, like Bett Southcott, this boy would eventually return home and resume some sort of place in the community, even if only as a supplicant for any state benefit going.

With his bulk went a strong feeling of lethargy: Oddie got the impression that what energy the boy had went into servicing his gross body – feeding it, putting clothes on it, propelling it around. The dull eyes, the absence of curiosity or even excitement about the events of the previous night, all suggested a torpor of intellect and spirit equal to the torpor of his body.

'They were all on at me to get my weight down,' he whined: 'the doc, the social workers, my parents . . . Never stopped nagging me.'

'Wouldn't it have been sensible to try?' Oddie asked.

Something close to strong emotion came into his face.

'It hurts! It's terrible wanting food and knowing you won't be eating for hours and hours, and then there won't be enough. And people like me never get any sympathy.'

'And that was why you left home?' asked WPC Gould, incredulous.

'That and other things . . . Well, that was the basic thing.'

Oddie tried another tack.

'How do you live?'

'Begging . . . People are mean to me, though.'

'You can't be eating as well as you used to do at home.'

'I manage. And I can eat what I want to.'

Shoplifting, thought Oddie. His clothes were still respectable enough not to make shop managers automatically suspicious. Probably shoplifting was the 'other thing' that had led to the breach with his family: they'd put him on short commons and he'd supplemented it from elsewhere.

'What can you tell me about what happened last night?'

'Nothing . . . Well, I heard all the others going down, so I followed. There was some sort of a scene going on next door, here I mean, but they were all crowding the doorway and I couldn't see properly. So I went back up to bed.' He paused, remembering, and then he brought out his real grievance: 'The police came and woke me up!'

Oddie had seldom had so strong a sense of death-in-life, of existence being stumbled through rather than lived.

When Charlie arrived back in Leeds he went straight to Portland Terrace. It was already after midday, and Alan was in the sitting room alone, eating a plate of toasted cheese and reading the morning paper.

'Katy's doing the shopping,' he said. 'We usually do it together, but we thought someone should be here.'

'I heard my boss in the front room as I came in. How is the questioning going?'

'They're getting through them. I don't suppose they're getting very much.'

'Why not?'

'Well, I was closest, wasn't I, and I was too late to see anything.'

'True.'

'And they tend to . . . keep out of things, if you know what I mean.'

'Keep out of things involving the police?'

'Yes. They wouldn't hurry when they heard the screams.'

'Does that mean they'd lie if they did see anything?'

'It might. But I doubt if they did.'

Charlie nodded. It made sense.

'Is there any news of . . . your father?'

Alan raised his eyebrows.

'Ben? I find it difficult to think of him as my father. The operation's over, he's still fighting, but it's touch and go. At least that's how I interpret what they told me on the phone. They're so cagey, and the language they use is so – I don't know – bland.'

'Hospitals have always been a bit like that.'

'It seems to make Ben into a *case*, not a human being.'

Charlie sat down and accepted a square of toasted cheese when Alan offered him the plate.

'How did you and Ben meet up again?'

'It wasn't again. We'd never met at all. He told me that almost the first thing. He's very honest, Ben.'

'He came looking for you, then?'

'That's right. He was waiting at the school gates – he'd asked someone to point me out. I was a bit suspicious at first.'

'I should think so.'

'But of course there were lots of others around, so there couldn't be a problem, and, well, I just looked at him, and he was explaining that he had something very important he wanted to talk to me about, and somehow I just knew he was on the level, knew it was important, and that he was going to be important in my life.'

Charlie could only think of what *might* have happened, remembering some of the child-molesters he had known.

'What did you do?'

'Went down to the St Mary's graveyard nearby, sat on one of the seats in the sun, and he told me he was my real father. You'd think I would have disbelieved him, thought he was having me on, but I didn't: I believed him right from the beginning. Ben's like that. You know you can trust him.'

Charlie, from his short conversation with Ben, could understand why Alan felt like that, dangerous though the feeling was. He hoped he was right.

'Did he explain about – well, your birth and that?'

'Oh yes. He was quite open. Said he had had a brief affair

with my mother, and that she must have married my father soon after I was born. "All credit to him", I remember him saying. "He's your father, and I'm not trying to take his place". He said he was young and irresponsible at the time.'

He would have been, Charlie estimated, in his mid twenties when Alan was born. Youngish, but hardly adolescent. He wondered whether Alan had done his mathematics.

'Did he say why he and your mother didn't marry, or try to make a go of the relationship?'

Alan shook his head, untroubled.

'Not really. Just said it didn't work out. But he said he was a bit of a Casanova, and he'd fathered other children. He said he thought one of them was also at Bramsey High.'

Charlie's brow was creased.

'I don't really see why he suddenly contacted you both.'

'Because he was back in the area. He'd been away for years – in Lincolnshire, then managing big estates first in Derbyshire, then near here. Recently he'd had a big lottery windfall, and he realized he'd got children walking the streets of Bramsey that he'd never seen. He said he'd sobered up a lot since his early days, but that thought really made him realize how irresponsible he'd been. Particularly as he was now working with homeless young people. It seemed to him that one day a kid might turn up at the door, and he'd find out that it was his own.'

'Out came the children running' – the line came to Charlie's mind from his schooldays.

All the little boys and girls,
something, something, something
Tripping and skipping, ran merrily after
The wonderful music with shouting and laughter.

But was the Pied Piper a benign or a malign figure? And what was Ben Marchant?

'Did he ask you to get in touch with Katy Bourne?'

'Oh no. That wouldn't have been right. He talked to her himself. But a couple of days later we all three went and had tea and cakes together in a café.' He thought seriously

122

about the experience. 'It was sort of odd, really. There was this girl who I'd never looked at twice at school, and she turned out to be my sister.'

'What did you talk about?'

'Oh, home, and school, and what we wanted to do when we left school. Ben talked about setting up the refuge, what he was trying to do here. Invited us round to see it.'

'Yes.'

Charlie had known he would do that. But was he using their adolescent enthusiasm and conscience as a bait, or just providing it with a natural outlet?

'And then, when he had to go and cook the meal here, Katy and I sat on for a bit talking, then we walked part of the way home together, and we –'

'Decided to leave home and come and work in the refuge?'

Alan shook his head vigorously.

'*No*. It wasn't like that at all. But we both felt we should have been told about Ben.'

'Did it occur to you that your mothers may have known very little, and none of it recent?'

'They could have told us what they knew. They could have told us the truth. But we didn't get all steamed up about it, and we didn't decide anything. It was just that . . . coming to help Ben was in the air.'

'And a sense of grievance, anger?'

Alan grinned.

'Something like that. Oh, I suppose we were over-reacting, but it's a big thing, finding your real father.'

'Of course it is.'

'So we went home feeling like that, and that evening I had it out with them – with Mum and Dad.'

'That must have been nasty.'

'Tearful, mostly. And Dad sort of embarrassed and blustery. I was still fuming the next day, and I rang Katy. And, well – you know the rest.'

'Your mum and dad will be worried at the moment.'

'Oh, I've rung them. I keep in touch, since we talked. Yes, they are worried, worried sick.'

'Wouldn't it be sensible to go home?'

123

Alan looked surprised.

'But how can I, even if I wanted to? Who would run the refuge? Ben will expect to find things in good order when he recovers.'

The last two residents of the Centre whom Oddie interviewed were at either end of its age spectrum. Tony he guessed was about thirteen or fourteen, and Oddie had to get a social worker to sit in on the interview. He also agreed to stay on for the formal interviews with Katy and Alan. Tony might be young, but he was fly. No amount of shock tactics or guile could get him to reveal his surname. At one point Oddie suspended the interview and got on the phone to police headquarters.

'I want the full name of any missing boys in the Yorkshire/ Lancashire area, aged around thirteen, with the Christian name Antony,' he demanded.

Tony didn't seem in the least concerned when the interview resumed.

'How do I spend my days?' he responded to Oddie's first question. 'Dodging you lot. It's a game, like. I can spot you coming a mile off. Pity you haven't got anything better to do.'

'Why do you want to dodge us?'

'Because you'd try to send me back home. Not that it would do any good. I'd be off and away again the next day.'

Oddie was sure this was true.

'What was so awful about home?' he asked.

Tony looked genuinely surprised.

'Home? Home wasn't awful. It was just dull. Nothing going on there. It's more exciting on the streets.'

'Doesn't it worry you, what can happen to you? Drugs? The sexual perverts? There's a lot of violence on the streets.'

'Don't you worry about me,' Tony said breezily. 'I can take care of myself. There's no one can put one over on me, or get me to do anything I don't want to do.'

'Why do you come to the hostel, then?'

'To have a bit of proper cooked food, a bit of a wash, and a good bed. This is my second time here. First time I didn't stay the whole fortnight. Got bored. Probably do the same this time. It's a bit of a break, that's all.'

'What about last night?'

'Oh – last night was exciting!'

But beyond giving a child's vividness to his account, Tony had nothing of substance to add.

The last resident made no bones about his name and age.

'Derek Redshaw, and I'm twenty-seven. Came here for the first time yesterday – wanting a bit of peace and quiet.'

He gave a sad, self-deprecating grin.

'Can get pretty violent among the people sleeping rough, I know,' agreed Oddie. But that wasn't his meaning.

'So-so. I can cope with that. I used to be in the army. I just wanted a bit of time to think things through, start making some decisions.'

'How come you left the army?'

'Didn't have any choice. I was invalided out. I'd been in the Gulf War and after that things were never the same. I had headaches, got neurotic, irritable, couldn't handle any sort of problem or emergency, fell out with everybody. There were a lot the same. And since they were cutting army numbers they were pleased to get rid of us.'

'Wasn't any help offered?'

'Not a great deal . . .' Suddenly a great hurt showed in his face. 'Tell you the truth, I couldn't believe how little. When you compared the propaganda hype we were given when we joined with what happened when they had no more use for us, it was disgusting. The army was, like, my family. My mother died when I was ten, and I was in a home after that. So I had nothing to come out to, and when the money ran out, that was it.'

'What about organizations like the British Legion?'

'As far as I'm concerned they're a lot of elderly wankers out for a boozy time.'

'Did you say this was your first day at the refuge?'

'That's right. First time I'd slept in a room for eighteen months or more. I was enjoying it. And I was thinking a lot, like I said. I felt I'd reached a turning point. I'd got myself together a bit in the last few months, and the headaches and the rages were less frequent. I was thinking about whether I was going to make an effort to get off the streets.'

'And were you?'

'I'd pretty much decided. Without being very sure what I could actually do about it, what sort of job I might go after. I'm just telling you this to explain why I didn't notice a great deal. I had my meal – pretty good it tasted too – and I met some of the others, but they were all a bit young, and in any case because I was thinking things through I'd spent the day in my room, and I went back there after supper.'

'Did you look out of the window?'

'Oh aye. Just idly. It was nice being on the inside looking out, instead of the outside looking in. Didn't stop me thinking. There's not a great deal going on in the street outside here – a right dead end.'

'But you saw, say, the people arrive who created a bit of a barney early in the evening?'

'I did. At least I saw the Indian chappie, but I didn't exactly see him arrive: I saw him park his car and come up the street. I'm in the attic, see, with the window built into the roof. It's not a splendid view – you certainly can't see the front door, or even the front gate. You can just see a bit of the road down from the house.'

'And Mrs Ingram – the woman with the red hair?'

'By then I was in the doorway of number twenty-two, enjoying the fun. I saw her arrive from there.'

'What about later: did you hear the screams?'

'Aye, I did – from a distance, but pretty horrifying.'

'Had you seen anything before that?'

'From the window?' He thought about it. He had, Oddie decided, a clear, hard, matter-of-fact brain that liked order. Eventually he was ready to reply. 'The light was failing by then. Hardly anybody about. Yes, there was someone who came up the street about then . . .'

'A woman with red hair?'

'She had a hat on. I couldn't see the hair, or the face. It was a blue hat with a small brim. And she was coming *up* the street, from Farnley Road.'

'You couldn't see if she came in?'

'No, I've told you: I couldn't see the gate.'

'But would the timing be about right if she'd come through the gate, let herself into the house, gone into the front room and stabbed the two, who then started screaming?'

He thought very hard.

'You're trying to put words into my mouth. I can't remember anything that contradicts that, but equally she may just have continued walking up the street.'

Oddie had to content himself with that.

When Katy came back from doing the shopping, and while Alan was putting it all away and making them a cup of coffee, Charlie talked to Katy about how Ben had suddenly come into her life.

'He came round to the house,' Katy said, sitting on the edge of her seat, obviously still excited by the memory. 'He'd seen Mum in the Bramsey Morrison's and followed her to the post office where she works part-time. Then he just looked in the telephone directory to find the C. Bourne who was closest to where she worked. I'd no sooner got in from school when he rang the doorbell. He must have been watching for me . . . He didn't even know my Christian name.'

'Not a very good start,' commented Charlie.

'It didn't seem like that. It seemed like we were beginning a voyage of discovery right from the very beginning.'

'Did you let him in?'

'Yes. I never had any doubts. I just looked at him and I *knew* he was nice and honest and not dangerous at all. He said, "I think I'm your father", and I looked at him and we both laughed – I don't laugh very often. And we sat in the front room and he talked about how he'd left Mum when she was pregnant and how it wasn't surprising if she felt bitter about it, and we talked about my life and what I wanted to do – only there wasn't much to say about *that*. And he said he had another child in the area – he was embarrassed about it, naturally – and I knew Alan by name. He said he was meeting him for tea the next day, and asked me to come too. It was like my life was suddenly being transformed. I said "Yes", but I wanted to dance for joy. And he said he hoped we wouldn't say anything to our parents yet, as it would be better if he approached them.'

'It probably would have been,' said Alan from the kitchen. 'I mucked that up. I felt so *angry* that I'd never been told that I blurted out that I knew.'

'That's when we decided to come here,' said Katy. 'We had had a wonderful tea with Ben. I was talking as I'd never talked before, and even with Alan alone afterwards it was – it was as if I'd been born again. Ben had given us the address, we knew the street, and then when Alan rang and said he'd had a bit of a bust-up with his parents and was thinking of going to live at the refuge, here, at least for a bit, I just said, "I'm coming too." And I've never regretted it, not for a moment.'

'It's not just being with Ben,' put in Alan. 'It's doing something really useful.'

'Yes, it's that,' agreed Katy, 'but it's also watching him, seeing how he deals with people, listens to them. It's not that I always agree with him. Sometimes I think he's too soft, but –'

The account was interrupted by a ring at the doorbell. As Alan went to answer it, Katy went on:

'It's probably someone wanting a room, someone who hasn't heard. It's a pity we can't take anybody today. I think Ben would want his room used as long as he's in hospital. We're going to see Mehjabean tonight, and we're hoping she can come back tomorrow. We want Ben to realize when he regains consciousness that we can cope, Alan and me. We really can. We –'

Alan reappeared at the doorway, standing awkwardly.

'Katy, it's your mother.'

CHAPTER 14

Parents and Children

If Alan had felt an awkwardness in announcing the visitor, that was nothing to the awkwardness that the visitor seemed to feel in getting herself through the door and into view of her daughter. The natural stiffness of the body was accentuated, and the hardness of the mouth and eyes were confused by an apparent realization that they ought to be softened, ought to be feeling something that they were not used to showing. To Charlie she looked like a very bewildered lady.

'Hello, Katy,' she said.

'Hello, Mum.'

There was a second's pause, then she rushed in.

'Katy, I've been worried sick since I heard the news on the radio. What have you got yourself into, girl?'

'There's no need to worry, Mum.'

'Now that plainly is nonsense, Katy,' said Mrs Bourne, conscious that in that at least reason was on her side. 'You have two vicious attacks in this house and you say there's nothing to worry about. It may be murder!'

'It wasn't people here,' said Katy, not looking at Charlie and hoping he would not contradict her. 'It was someone who came from outside.'

'I don't see what difference that makes. Someone came in and tried to murder your . . . your father. I think that should tell you something about him.'

Katy's chin went up – a characteristic gesture, born of opposition.

'It doesn't tell me anything at all. It's not a crime to be

murdered,' said Katy, clearly feeling that the balance of reason had shifted to her side.

'Your father's gone through life thinking he can do what he pleases and bugger the consequences for anybody else. He hasn't cared who he hurt. I want you to come home, Katy.'

A mulish expression came into Katy's eyes.

'I can't come home. Alan and I are going to keep this place running until Ben comes out.'

Reluctantly Mrs Bourne turned to Charlie.

'Tell her that's just not on, *please*. They're teenagers, for God's sake.'

'We're not happy with the situation here,' said Charlie, speaking reluctantly. 'But there are limits to what we can do. Say we were to order Katy and Alan home. What's to keep them there if they don't want to stay?'

'I'd bloody lock her in if necessary!'

'Your house hardly looked like San Quentin to me. She'd be out of the window the moment you went to work.' He saw that she acknowledged the truth of this. 'What I'd suggest –'

'Yes?' She seemed willing to grasp at any suggestion.

'At the moment Alan and Katy are perfectly safe. The two houses are swarming with policemen. I suggest that what you need is time to talk things over quietly with Katy. And I don't think here is the place – or now the time, either, come to that, with things going on everywhere. What you need is an absence of fuss. I suggest that Katy comes to see you tomorrow, and you begin to talk things through.'

'But she'll try to make me come home,' protested Katy, aware that she sounded childish.

'Your mother's perfectly justified in being concerned, and she's got a right to try to persuade you to return home. Will you go and talk to her?'

There was a silence.

'I suppose so,' said Katy. 'But I'm not going home.'

'Well, that seems to be the best you can do,' said Mrs Bourne, grudgingly. Then she tried to right herself. 'I do miss you, Katy. You may have thought I wouldn't, but I do.'

'You miss the shopping and cleaning and cooking I did.'

'All right. I miss all that. But I miss you, too.'

She turned and went out with rather more dignity than she had brought in with her. At least she did not try to feign surprise at the unforgivingness of the young. Charlie followed her into the hall.

'It *was* the best I could do.'

'Yes. I . . . I'm sorry if I sounded ungrateful.'

'You may find you have to share her with this place. It's captured her imagination.'

'Whatever's happened to "A daughter's a daughter for the rest of your life?"' Mrs Bourne demanded, the grievance back in her voice.

Charlie shook his head in wonderment. Where did such people live?

'That hasn't been true for a long time, if it ever was. Daughters grow up, get jobs, move away just like sons these days. When I spoke to you before you didn't seem concerned at losing your daughter.'

'No . . .' She hesitated, looking down at the carpet. 'I missed her, much more than I expected to. Losing her to her father is pretty hard, after all that happened.'

'I've been talking to someone today who's in pretty much the same position as you, and she doesn't seem to feel any bitterness – says Ben always made it clear to her that he wasn't the marrying kind.'

'Bully for her. I bet she's got help in bringing it up.'

'She's got her mother.'

'There you are.'

'But the child is a spastic.'

The argument fell on stony ground. The aggressive sense of grievance came into her eyes again.

'I suppose you want me to think there's always someone worse off than yourself? I'm not that philosophical.'

'Did Ben promise you marriage, or pressure you to have the child?'

She looked down.

'Well, I may have misled you a bit there. You've been fair to me today, and I'll try to be fair with you. He did say he'd try to have a long-term relationship, but he also said he wasn't the type for it, and that it'd be hard. It was me decided to have the child, because I thought it would help me to keep him. Aren't we women daft? It was when I'd decided to have it that he encouraged me, said it would be loved and so on. But not, unfortunately, by him. He took off before it was born, like I said.'

'You seem to bear a grudge – quite understandably.'

She looked at him, animal cunning in her eyes.

'If you think that fifteen years later I upped and – what was it? – cut his throat, you're out of your mind.'

'What were you doing last night around ten o'clock?'

'Sitting home feeling a bit lonesome and watching telly. Ken Wade, the man who runs my pub quiz team, rang some time then. I expect you could check with British Telecom.'

'We'll do that.'

'But I'll tell you one thing: you're barmy to think I could have done it, after all these years, but you're right there'll be a woman in it somewhere. I don't say she'll have done it, not cut his throat, but she'll either be behind it, or be the cause. Because Ben and women, together, they're dynamite. That's one reason I don't want Katy staying on here. After all, she can't *think* of him as her father, can she?'

'What is it about Ben Marchant that makes him so irresistible?' asked Charlie, genuinely curious. 'He seemed a quiet, sincere, concerned bloke to me.'

'Whatever he's doing at the time, he makes it seem the biggest thing on earth. Nothing else matters, everything centres on that one interest. And if it's you that's the interest – wow!'

'But if he drops you –'

'*When* he drops you, then it's the end of the world. It was for me. This attack here, it'll be because of some woman whose world has crumbled around her.'

Alan and Katy very much wanted to go together to see Mehjabean that evening, but they weren't happy at leaving the refuge unstaffed.

'I suppose it doesn't matter,' said Alan to Charlie, 'with all the policemen around. But if anybody comes looking for a room, it gives a terrible impression.'

'We do,' agreed Charlie, whose irony went unappreciated. 'Why don't you leave Derek in charge?'

'Derek?'

'The chap in the attic of number twenty-two. He's a bit older than the rest, and seems a capable chap,' said Charlie, who had talked to Oddie about him and taken a cup of coffee with him in his room, with devious intent.

'Oh yes. He only came yesterday, and I hardly saw anything of him, though my room's opposite his. Well, if you think he could cope . . .'

By the time they left they were sure he could cope. He told them that he would just do for any refuge-seeker what they'd done for him the day before, except that he'd tell them there might be a room the next day. Otherwise he'd stick around in the living room of number twenty-four and try to help with any problems. He made no fuss about it – just like Ben.

The hospital, in the centre of Leeds behind the town hall, was all bustle and light – very different from the Centre, until you looked closer and saw the cheap, shoddy uniforms, the overcrowding, the air of harassment and just-about-coping. The news about Ben was a little more encouraging. The attack had been vicious but wild, and had been too low to be totally effective. Ben was not out of danger, but his condition was stable.

'How can you call it stable if he still might die?' Katy asked.

She was told that he was getting no worse, and if he could maintain that condition he would be out of danger. There was no question of the police interviewing him for quite a while yet.

At Mehjabean's bedside there was a visitor – a substantial middle-aged man whom they realized must be her father. When she saw them come through the curtain pulled aside by the policeman who was currently guarding her, Midge's face lit up. Her father looked round nervously, got up from his chair and, after a brief greeting or rather nod to his daughter's friends, took off. Alan raised an eyebrow at Midge.

'What was he trying to do?'

'Oh, nothing really,' said Midge, trying to speak without moving her jaw too much. 'He says the marriage is definitely off. I told him it was never on, as far as I was concerned.'

'Do you believe him?'

'I *think* so . . . I told him that the wound was going to leave a permanent scar and he *seemed* concerned for me, rather than for my prospects.'

'Oh *Midge*!' cried Katy. 'How awful! But surely with plastic surgery –'

Midge grinned, then flinched.

'I was testing him. You don't think any doctor would commit himself so soon, do you? They're worse than lawyers. At the moment I'm in the dark, and they probably are too.'

'If the marriage is off, how is your dad going to cope with his financial problems?' Alan asked.

'He says he's found a buyer for two of his shops. If those deals go through, the pressure would be off.'

Katy thought.

'But aren't all his shops run by members of your family?'

'Yes. I expect they'll be pretty sore at me.'

That thought hung in the air for a moment, and Alan was not changing the subject when he said:

'You'll be coming back to live at Portland Terrace, won't you, Midge?'

'Oh yes. Tomorrow, they say. Are there lots of gorgeous policemen around?'

'I don't know about gor –' Alan began.

'They *feel* gorgeous,' said Katy. 'In the circumstances.'

'I'll be as safe there as anywhere then,' said Mehjabean. 'When the whole thing's solved, then we will have to rethink. Maybe Ben will be well enough to advise by then. Maybe I'll be ready to go back to my family.'

'It sounds as if Ben's recovery will take a while,' said Alan, sombrely. 'It could be a long while, in fact he may never recover.'

'Well, the case could take a while too,' said Midge. 'Though that's not a cheerful prospect.' She frowned, in thought. 'I *wish* I could remember something – something that the police would find useful. Something to say whether it was a man or a woman, for example. It seems so feeble to have to say that the attack just sort of descended on us out of the blue, without our having any idea of who it was, what kind of person. But that's the truth. All I remember is the sudden pain, and keeling forward to cradle my face. And when they come to question him, I really don't think Ben will remember anything more than me.'

'But I do think you should try to remember more,' said Alan urgently. 'Or perhaps not *try*, but leave your mind blank, and hope that some memory will suddenly come in.'

'That's the sort of thing people say,' said Mehjabean with a touch of scorn. 'If I try to let my mind go blank all my troubles and worries and dangers come jostling along for space.'

It was a rare complaint, a rare glimpse of her state of mind. But Alan pressed on.

'You ought to try. You read about these cases where suddenly someone remembers something – something light as a feather – and they nearly don't mention it to the police, but they do, and it leads to other things, and that's how they get the murderer.'

'Sounds more like murder in a book,' said Midge sceptically. 'Most murders in real life seem to be solved by P C Plod going round from door to door asking Mrs Jones and Mrs Smith if they saw anything on their way to the shops.'

But after Alan and Katy had gone, something in what had been said troubled Midge, yet refused to come to the conscious forefront of her mind.

Oddie had delegated the initial questioning of the Haldalwa family to D C Iqbal, an Urdu-speaking policeman whom they had borrowed for the occasion from Keighley. He had gone about his business with commendable dispatch, and came to present his initial report to Oddie at the refuge that same evening.

'The women are easy,' he said. 'They were all at home with their children, except one aunt of Mehjabean who was visiting another aunt, with her children. All were watching

135

television, or hired videos of the exploits of heroic princes and lovers, from the Hollywood of the East. I presume you're not really interested in the women?'

'Open mind,' said Oddie. 'Don't presume anything.'

'Right you are. But I didn't get the impression they had anything to hide. Then the men. They were all, except one, at a meeting at Razaq Haldalwa's. They were hearing that he was going to sell some of his businesses. It was a heated meeting.'

'And the one exception?'

'He was minding his shop. He couldn't get anyone to stand in for him – it was his wife who was out. There won't be any problem establishing his alibi, I wouldn't think.'

'No,' said Oddie thoughtfully. 'The funny thing is, I prefer the alibi of the one who was alone in his shop to the alibis of all those men together at Razaq Haldalwa's.'

Charlie was in quest of Ben Marchant's past. It was not that he ruled out the residents of the Centre as suspects – far from it. But it seemed to him that it was equally likely that the man's extraordinary past – scattering in his wake children for which he accepted no responsibility – played some part in provoking the murder attack. Nor could a link with the refuge dwellers be ruled out: Ben Marchant himself had toyed with the possibility of one of his own children turning up at the refuge. Granted the home background of many of the young homeless, that would not be too outrageous a coincidence.

Ben's previous employers could possibly be a fruitful source of information, but, confident as Charlie was, he felt he ought to be with Oddie when talking to local grandees, even if they were, as Mrs Ingram implied, of the newly rich variety. Meanwhile, with an evening to himself, he decided to talk to Alan's parents.

Mrs Coughlan was up and bustling, and the living room was tidy and polished to a sparkle. It got enough of the evening sun to seem quite pleasant this time round. Mrs Coughlan was obviously the mover in the household, and

Arthur Coughlan the passive, despondent and altogether lesser partner in the marriage.

The phrase Mrs Coughlan used to sum up her feelings was the same as Mrs Bourne's, but totally appropriate for all that.

'I'm worried sick,' she said. 'We both are.'

'Rose can't stop talking about it,' said Arthur, 'and if I went down the Railway it would be the same. Was it one of those dossers that done it, Mr Peace?'

'We don't know,' said Charlie, sitting down in the same fat armchair as he had used previously and trying to establish an atmosphere of confidentiality. 'It's very early days yet. It's possible that Ben Marchant got a glimpse of the attacker, and will tell us who it was when he can talk. That won't be for a day or two yet, if ever.'

'You mean he might die?' asked Rose Coughlan.

'It's still very possible. Would that upset you?'

She bridled a little.

'Oh, not in the way you mean. But he is Alan's father, when all's said and done. No, what worries me is it'll be murder then, won't it? And having Alan stay in that house . . .'

'I'm afraid the attack was so savage that there's really very little difference between murder and attempted murder. The intent was definitely there, though there may have been some wavering at the last minute. As to Alan staying on there, I've done my best, but he's determined. They both are. And with so many policemen in the house and around it, he's as safe there as he would be here.'

Mrs Coughlan was reluctant to accept that.

'But will the police be there until he's caught?'

'I hope so. And I hope it will be soon. But why are you assuming that it's a he? With Ben Marchant's record, wouldn't it be more likely to be a she?'

'Record?' Mrs Coughlan had misunderstood him for a moment. 'Oh, sorry: I thought you meant criminal record. I don't know as he's ever had that.'

'Should have been chased for maintenance several times over if the Child Support Agency knew what they were at,' said Arthur Coughlan.

'I never harassed him for money,' said his wife, looking at his aggrieved face. 'Alan was only three months when we married, and you had a good enough job.'

'*Then*,' said Arthur bitterly. 'And it was never a high payer, so we never had another of our own. Alan was *our* child . . . till *he* came along.'

'He still is,' said Charlie. 'He's told me he can never regard Ben as his father. You are.'

The gloom lightened, but only momentarily, on Arthur's face.

'Then what's the bloody attraction?' he demanded.

'Of Ben? I think the fact that he's doing good. And he is a very charismatic person, in a quiet way.'

'Does that mean attractive, like?' Rose Coughlan asked. 'He was always that, and quiet too. So quiet you thought he was sincere, believed what he told you.'

'Do you think, now, that you were silly to believe what he told you?' asked Charlie.

'Not exactly that . . .' She sat in thought. 'It's difficult, it being so long ago. I hadn't thought about Ben for years, except sometimes looking at Alan and seeing something of him . . . I think often he believed what he was saying. And often he would be honest, like he'd make no bones about being faithful and that. He wasn't faithful by nature, and he'd say so. But he could also say "I love you" as if he meant it, and you always felt that, maybe . . . maybe you *would* prove to be the one.'

'You hoped so,' said Charlie gently.

'Oh yes. At the time I hoped so, so *much*.'

'How do you see him now?'

'I think there must have been good in him – *be* good in him, still. Good intentions. But he always had to have what he wanted, and he didn't care how he got it.'

'You mean women?'

She shook her head.

'Well, I don't mean only that. Women were important to him, but mainly for . . . the obvious.' She looked down into her lap. 'He always had lots of other interests, and there'd always be one big, mastering idea. Something he was going

138

all out for. And when he'd got it, well, then he'd need something new to chase after. It was like he'd hop from flower to flower, not just with women, but with ideas, ambitions.'

'Do you think this refuge for the homeless may be like that, just one of his flowers?'

'Oh, I *hope* so!' She immediately looked ashamed. 'Sorry – seems heartless, to say that. I'm sorry for those young people – it breaks my heart to see lives thrown away like that. And maybe he has grown up, grown older and wiser, so that he will keep on and make a go of it. But I don't want Alan there.'

'That's natural, but he *is* doing good work,' Charlie pointed out, 'not just playing.'

'He needs to be studying, going to college, settling on some sort of work he wants to do later in life.'

'He's probably thinking a lot about that while he's working at the Centre.'

'It's his summer holiday! He should be having a good time before he starts work for his A-levels.'

'I think in his way he is having a good time.'

'He may be doing that and still be being used. I don't want to speak ill of Ben when he's so sick, but have you ever thought he's using his children now just like he used his women in the past? Have you thought maybe that's the only kind of relationship he knows?'

CHAPTER 15

Employers

'I'll keep a low profile,' said Charlie, as they drove out to the Mallabys of Belstone Manor next morning.

'Oh? Why?'

'I have an idea they'll be old-fashioned Tory types who won't be easy with the idea of a black policeman.'

'Maybe. That wasn't quite how Mrs Ingram saw them, was it? Anyway, keep an open mind. When Mrs Ingram and her recognition of Marchant comes up, you'll have to take over anyway. You're the one who talked to her.'

They were taking the scenic route from Leeds to Otley, and, having driven through Cookridge, were now passing rolling farmland as they approached the Chevin.

'People around here must have a bob or two,' commented Charlie.

'A bob or two, a million or two,' said Oddie, shrugging. 'Farmers aren't quite on the gravy train they used to be on, but Mallaby isn't a farmer, as I understand it, or only as a sideline. He's a businessman.' He thought. 'Rather Victorian that: retreating from your place of business to play at being landed gentry in the lush countryside.'

When they finally arrived at Belstone Manor, the Victorian comparison was reinforced by cast-iron gates and the gate-house beside them. However, the latter looked empty, and you gained admittance by ringing and stating your business into a speaking device. The voice which asked it sounded landed – no butler, presumably. When Oddie said, 'West Yorkshire police', the gates swung open and Charlie drove them through.

'Jane Austen meets James Bond,' he commented.

The house was early nineteenth-century and heavily gracious – rather like Alicia Ingram. The front door was opened by Sir George himself, and he shook hands heartily.

'Only got some new Filipinos,' he explained, as if they were a breed of watchdog. 'Awfully sweet and wonderful about the house, but no good with the telephone or callers. So I prefer to do it myself. If you'll come through to the drawing room.'

He led the way down the high hall to a sunny room in which the French windows, a recent innovation apparently, looked out on to the garden. Sir George was hearty, friendly (Charlie had detected no reaction to his colour) and moustached in the style of a country gentleman rather than a serviceman. He was a little too small to be the ideal bluff countryman, but he worked to make up for the deficiency.

'You said you'd like to speak to my wife, too, didn't you?' He went to the windows, opened them and bellowed: 'Susan!' He turned and gestured them to large, square armchairs, new or newly covered in a traditional style. The men saved effort by waiting until his wife arrived before they sat down, and Sir George filled in time. 'No help to be got for the garden these days. Can't fly in Filipinos for that. We have a man two afternoons a week, and Susan does the rest.'

Susan, it turned out, was more effortlessly the picture of the country gentlewoman of a certain age. Her hair was drawn back into a bun, but quite a lot of it had escaped and now hung around her wide forehead. She wore a capacious, smock-like dress, thick dark stockings and heavy shoes. She left a fork and trowel on a window-ledge and came breezing in.

'Hello. I'm filthy, so I won't shake hands. This time of year it's never ending out there. Now, you're the policemen and it's about Ben, isn't it? When we heard the name on the news we wondered if you'd be wanting to talk to us. Awful thing – horrible! How is he, poor old chap?'

'Holding his own,' said Oddie. 'But it's still touch and go.'

'He didn't deserve that,' she said, sitting down in a billow of flowery cotton, and letting them get a glimpse of sturdy

141

calf. Charlie, sitting, opened his book. For the moment he was the note-taker. 'After all the good he was trying to do,' said Lady Mallaby, resuming the subject of Ben. 'Do you think it was one of his street people? A lot of them are sad creatures, but there are some out-and-out weirdos as well.'

'We're keeping an open mind,' said Oddie, with a finality that said he'd ask the questions. 'Now, Ben Marchant was your estate manager, I believe. How long did he work for you?'

Sir George took over the answering.

'Five years. I've looked him up in the farm file since you rang. He came in the spring of '91.'

'I believe he'd worked in Derbyshire somewhere. Did he come to you from there?'

'That's right. Somewhere near Matlock. I think he'd been there since finishing Agricultural College.'

'And he came with good references?'

'Excellent. And deserved them. If he'd needed references when he left I'd have given him glowing ones.'

'I see. Farming is a sort of –' Oddie nearly said hobby, but thought that sounded insulting – 'sideline with you, sir, isn't it? You're actually an industrialist.'

There was no hesitancy in Sir George's nod.

'That's right. In so far as the country has any industry left. Sabre Industries plc. Ben had nothing to do with that. But if you're implying that I don't know what I'm doing in the farming line, then you're wrong. I was brought up in farming countryside in North Yorkshire. I know the business – and it is a business these days – inside out. And you can believe me when I tell you that Ben was a damned good farm and estate manager.'

'I'm sure he was,' said Oddie placatingly. 'I was just trying to gauge the amount of responsibility he had. I take it he was basically in charge of the whole farming operation.'

'Yes – the smallish farm that we run ourselves, and then the financial and organizational supervision of the tenant farmers of the rest of the estate. I never had a moment's worry the whole time he was here: he knew what he was doing, and he was honest.'

'What about his private life?'

Sir George shot him a glance.

'We're not running a monastery here. His private life was his own affair.'

'Of course it was. Less so now he's been stabbed, though. I'm not asking you to make judgements. I just want information.'

'Oh tell him, George,' said Susan Mallaby impatiently. 'There was Hattie Jenkins, wife of one of the tenant farmers, Mrs Gregson who runs a hat shop in Otley, and Sally Wormold who has the village shop and post office. There may be more, of course, but those are the ones there were rumours about.'

'Children?'

Lady Mallaby smiled knowingly.

'Hardly. They were all married women, some of them with older children or grown-up ones, and well able to take care of that kind of thing. Mrs Gregson would have been past the age, I'd guess. No, there was little danger of that.'

'I ask because there had been children in the past.'

'Out of wedlock? Oh dear, I betray my age. Nobody uses that term now, do they? I suppose Ben was just ahead of his time. Wasn't there something at one time, George, about a letter from the Child Support Agency?'

'That's right,' said her husband. 'Got it in my mail. Get a great big bundle every day here. His address was The Lodge, Belstone Manor. Easy mistake for the postman to make. Anyway, I just opened it without looking.' His face took on a roguish expression. 'A bit of a shock, at my age.'

'A bit of a miracle, more like,' said his wife.

'Anyway, I just sealed it down with Sellotape and put "opened in error" on it and put it in his door on my way out.'

'He never commented on it?'

'Never.'

'And you didn't see any of the details? The name of the child or its mother?'

'If I did it's gone now. And it can't have meant anything to me, so it won't have been local.'

'No natural curiosity, men,' commented Lady Mallaby tartly.

Oddie shot a covert glance at Charlie, who sat forward in his chair.

'This may seem like a change of subject, but it's not,' he said, looking at Lady Mallaby. 'I believe you know a Mrs Ingram.'

'Do I? Doesn't ring a bell. What's her Christian name?'

'Alicia.'

'Is she one of the people on the Leeds Piano Competition Committee, George?'

'Haven't the foggiest, m'dear. "Chopsticks" with two fingers is about my limit.'

'You don't have to *play*, George.' She thought hard. 'I have a feeling she is. Is she a frightfully condescending type – "I am trying desperately hard to bring myself down to your level" when she talks to you?'

'Er . . . people might react like that to her manner,' said Charlie.

'Active in Conservative Party circles?'

'Yes, certainly.'

'I've got her. Yes, she's been here. Muscled her way on to the committee without any particular qualifications.'

'When would this have been, when she came here?'

'Oh, a while ago. Let me see: maybe two years. We only met here because the original venue became unavailable at the last minute and I suggested there was room here.'

'I ask because I believe when the meeting broke up, you all came out to the entrance hall, and Sir George and Ben Marchant were talking there.'

Lady Mallaby shot him a piercing glance.

'Good Lord! You seem to know more about our activities than we remember ourselves. Have you had surveillance cameras out here for the last two years? It's positively spooky!'

'Actually there's no mystery about it,' said Charlie hurriedly. 'I got the information from Mrs Ingram herself. What I wondered was whether you remember the incident and whether you noticed her reaction to the sight of Ben Marchant.'

'I think I may be of help to you there,' said Sir George. 'I remember the occasion because I noticed a woman reacting to him.' He became slightly roguish again. 'Tell you the truth, I often did notice Ben's effect on women. Those women that Susan mentioned, the women around here, if ever they and Ben came in contact you could *tell*, if you were sharp. And other women who fancied him – well, I'm sure I don't have to spell it out.'

'Sex quite frequently rears its ugly head in our job, Sir George,' said Charlie urbanely.

'All the time, I should think. Anyway, I remember the committee coming out into the hall, and I recall this woman – I had no idea who she was, still haven't – catching sight of Ben, and her jaw dropping just for a moment. Quite dramatic, like a stage play. Then she covered it up – very practised, good at putting on an act, that one. I'm assuming that will have been Mrs Ingram.'

'Did you guess what was the cause of the reaction?'

Sir George stroked his jaw.

'I suppose I put it down to her being a former lady friend of Ben's. No evidence, none at all. I suppose it's just the obvious thing to think in the circumstances.'

'Obvious generally, or obvious because the man was Ben Marchant?'

'Because it was Ben.'

'Were you surprised when Marchant won the lottery?'

It was Oddie, taking over the questioning from Charlie. Sir George turned to him.

'Surprised? I suppose one is always surprised when someone one knows gets a big win.'

'Would you have said he was the lottery type?'

Sir George frowned.

'I knew he bought tickets. He often mentioned it, and I remember him being quite jealous when one of the estate workers won twenty-five pounds. And I once saw him coming out of the newsagents down in the village and scratching one of those damned cards. I do think they are beyond the pale, don't you? Whole thing's a bit iffy, if you ask me.'

'So he was the type.'

'Optimistic, a bit short-term – yes, I'd say so.'

'Always waiting for something to turn up?'

Sir George balked a little at that.

'That would be a bit unfair, because Micawber was a hopeless case. Ben was like a lot of people, hoping something would turn up, while going very competently about his daily business.'

Oddie nodded his acceptance of this analysis.

'So tell me what happened when he got his big win.'

'Let me see . . .' Sir George looked at his wife. 'It was you he told first, wasn't it, dear?'

'Yes. I was driving out to the village one Sunday morning to get the papers – no delivery here – and he waved me down and crowed that he'd got a big win in the lottery draw the night before. I was pleased for him, and I said, "Come up and have a drink before lunch". Which he did.'

'Did he say how much it was?'

'I'm not sure that you know at once, do you? Anyway, he didn't say, either then or later, did he, George?'

'Not to me. Just used words like "substantial", "considerable", and suchlike. I never heard anyone name a sum, not one that they'd actually heard from him.'

'Did you guess a sum?'

'Well, I suppose he bought those two houses – they'd be in the thirty thousand range. So I thought it must be over a hundred thousand, remembering he was feeding these people, and so on. I suspected it would be double that, or a quarter of a million. But this was only guesswork. It could be many millions for all I know, except that Ben never said it was a top prize. But then nobody sensible *would* tell people if it was that sort of sum they'd won, would they?'

'I suppose not,' agreed Oddie. 'When did he announce his plans to set up this refuge?'

'Almost from the first.' He looked at his wife. 'I say "almost" because I can't remember whether he told us when he came up for that Sunday drink. I know he said he'd be chucking in his job here, because that's when I realized it was a real win, not just glorified small change.'

'I think it was a few days later that he told you,' said Lady Mallaby. 'I seem to remember we discussed it over dinner.'

'How did you react to the idea?'

'Me? It wasn't my business. It was his money and his to do what he wanted with. Nobody can walk through the streets of Leeds or London and not wonder a bit about what has happened to the country. I suppose what we thought was that it was a wonderful idea and very generous, but that the money wouldn't last for ever. That was pretty much our reaction, wasn't it, George?'

'So far as I recall, yes. I suppose I was a bit surprised because I'd always thought of Ben as a country person, and kids on the streets are a town problem, if you get my drift.'

'Was Ben a country person by birth?'

'Now that you mention it, I think not. Leeds, I think. So he was going home.'

'When I asked you how you reacted to Ben's idea, I really meant: did it seem to you to be in character? Did it follow on from anything you knew about him?'

They looked at each other, rather at a loss.

'I think so,' said Sir George slowly. 'There was a high degree of concern for the environment. Hedgerows, anti-battery hens, that sort of thing. A bit schoolchildish, if that doesn't sound too nasty. Nature and farming have always had their brutal sides. And then he always had a great interest in children. We sometimes have school parties out to the farm – told them a thing or two about what we were doing, then gave them the freedom of the place. Ben always enjoyed that.'

'But you say he never talked about his own children?'

'Never. I'm right, aren't I, Susan?'

'Oh, absolutely. Apart from the CSA letter, I had no idea. Though now I come to think about it, I did get a notion once –'

'Yes?'

She sat for a moment in thought.

'It was just watching Ben once, with one of the farm

147

workers. They have a spastic child, and I saw Ben with it, and he was so . . . so tender, and loving and concerned that I *did* wonder if he'd had such a child. It was just a guess. It was probably nothing more than Ben being Ben. He was – sorry, is – naturally a concerned person. Always *involved* with whatever he was doing.'

'It was a good guess, as a matter of fact, Lady Mallaby . . . By the way, where were you both two nights ago – the night Marchant was stabbed?'

'I was here,' said Sir George. 'Check with our Filipinos, if you can make them understand. Oh, and one of our tenant farmers, Alf Arden, was here about half past nine.'

'And I was at a Conservative Party do at the Royal in Leeds,' said Susan Mallaby. 'Can't think why – politics has no appeal these days. But there'll be plenty of people you can check it with.'

'Well, I don't think I have any more questions.' Oddie looked at Charlie, who briefly shook his head. 'If you should think of anything, either of you, any little thing that could be of relevance, please call us at once.'

'Of course,' said Sir George.

'I take it from your questions,' said his wife, 'that you are looking outside the refuge for your attacker?'

'We're looking both outside and inside,' said Oddie carefully. 'It seems the attacker may have left by the front door, but that tells us precisely that and little more. It doesn't rule out people from the second house, or even people from number twenty-four, because they could have come back in in the confusion. All options are still open. Obviously we have to remember that Marchant has a life outside the refuge, and a past as well as a present.'

'He is a good man,' said Susan Mallaby stoutly. 'Past or no past.'

As they drove out of the gates Oddie said: 'Ring road, and then quickest way back to Leeds.' Charlie nodded, and turned left to the village. It was two miles from the Manor, was called Monkton, and it had a village shop that fulfilled the multiple function of newsagents, general store and post office.

'One of Marchant's ladyfriends runs that, I suppose,' said Oddie. 'And here's the pub. They'll be discussing Ben Marchant here, I'll be bound.'

It was nearly lunchtime, and outside the Black Heifer there was indeed a knot of what looked like locals, drinking in the sun and deep in conversation.

'One thing,' said Charlie, then stopped for thought.

'Spit it out.'

'You talked about Ben having a past as well as a present. But thinking about the present: so far we haven't had any suggestion of a lady friend in the Bramsey area, or anywhere else, at the moment.'

'Too busy, maybe.'

'With his past, does it sound likely that he wouldn't have a woman, however busy he was?'

'Maybe not . . . No, you're right. Do you think Alan and Katy know and aren't telling, or just don't know?'

'Shouldn't be too hard to find out . . . The lottery story sounded OK as they told it.'

'Yes. Or really you mean as *he* told it to *them*. He may have been having them on.'

'Of course. Though it's difficult to see why.'

'Any number of reasons if he'd come by the money in some illegal or dubious way. Anyway, it's something that has to be checked. Not something I've ever done before, though I don't suppose they will make any difficulties. Would you like to investigate possible girlfriends while I get on to Camelot? Camelot! What a name! The modern version of the holy grail – a lottery win.'

Charlie nodded his acceptance. In fact the possible girl-friend was only one of several avenues that he felt minded to explore.

CHAPTER 16

The Final Girlfriend

When they got back to Leeds, Charlie dropped Oddie off at police headquarters, then drove off once again to Portland Terrace. The scene-of-crime people had finished now and had departed with their bagged loot of dust, mud and blood specimens. The place should have been regaining an air of normality, but just one policeman on the door was enough to prevent that. Inside, however, there was only a single representative of the law tucked away in each house, and in number twenty-four Charlie found Derek putting the dining room to rights.

'I don't know that anyone will fancy eating here tonight,' he said dubiously. 'Katy was talking in terms of a fork meal, which is probably sensible. Still, we've got to come back in here some time, and nobody's dead.'

'Nobody's dead yet.'

'The kids have had a message from the hospital. They can go and see Ben, but he won't be able to talk to them.'

'Great,' said Charlie, unenthusiastically. 'I suppose that means we can go and question him in Morse code.'

'He may be up to writing his answers. Or you could ask him questions that need a yes or no answer, and he could make signs,' Derek suggested. 'Do I gather that Ben is a long-lost father, suddenly reappeared out of the blue, for Katy and Alan?'

'Very much so.'

'Bit too like a bloody fairy story for my taste.'

'Are they around?'

'Upstairs in Katy's room, discussing what they'll say to

him. They're very excited – over the moon, in fact. Otherwise most people have gone back to take up their begging positions, and to dispute them if anyone's tried to take them over.'

Charlie lingered in the doorway.

'Do I detect a note of scorn?'

'For the kids? Not a bit. I used to play my mouth organ – "Tunes You Have Loved" – and sell the *Big Issue*, and I used to tell myself it wasn't begging. But it was only a step or two up, wasn't it? No, if there's scorn it's for the politicians. What a way to treat our young people. And even if they're not sleeping rough but mooching around all day – what a load of trouble they're storing up for the future.'

'Yeah – and look who'll be carrying the can and mopping up the trouble,' said Charlie bitterly.

He shut the door and went softly up the stairs. Going softly was a good idea if you were a policeman, and if you could manage it. There was a threadbare carpet on the stairs, carefully laid. Ben must be quite a handyman. On the landing WPC Gould was sitting. Charlie nodded to her, but went in the direction of the voices he could hear.

'Obviously we'll talk to him about Mehjabean,' Alan was saying in his nearly adult voice, in the bedroom at the end of the corridor. 'But maybe not too much. And of course we'll say that things are fine here at the refuge.'

'Well, they *are*,' said Katy defensively.

'As fine as they can be with policemen everywhere. And then should we say we'll stay here for as long as necessary?'

'Of course,' said Katy, simply and finally.

'Yes. It's what Ben would want, and it's what we want too ... Lucky it coincides, isn't it?' The next words came more uncertainly. 'Do you think we need help?'

Katy was silent for a moment.

'Well, we might. If we got anyone like Mouse again. Or Mouse himself, trying to come back ... I wish it was Mouse that did it, Alan.'

'Maybe it was. But even if he was carted off, there's more like him out there.'

'But we've got Derek now, and there are others – Zak, for example: he'd help us.'

'Zak's fine, but I'm not sure that in a crisis . . .'

Charlie thought it was time to interrupt. He knocked on the door and went in.

'They've told us we can see Ben,' Alan said excitedly, as if that was all that mattered.

'So I hear. Maybe we'll be able to talk to him too.' He sat down with them on the bed. 'Tell me, how long have you two been at the refuge now?'

They had to screw their minds back to answer the question.

'Three, nearly four weeks,' said Alan, after counting.

'That's about what I thought. I suppose for Ben it was pretty much a full-time job, wasn't it?'

'Oh yes. We're still at the stage of setting it up and getting it known.'

'So he was here twenty-four hours a day, mostly?'

'Not necessarily,' said Katy. 'There were people to see, people who could help, or people who were making trouble: local councillors, that sort of thing. And of course he had to have a bit of time to himself.'

'What sort of thing would he do with that time?' Charlie asked.

'Mostly he'd go to the pub,' Alan said.

'How often?'

'Maybe two or three times a week.'

'You didn't go with him?'

'Of course not. We're under age. Anyway, there had to be someone here.'

'Do you think he really went there?'

'What do you mean?' Alan said, indignantly, getting a little red. 'You don't think we tried to smell his breath, do you? That's the sort of thing my mum would do if I'd been at a party – thought she could do it so's I wouldn't notice.'

'What I'm wondering,' said Charlie carefully, 'is whether Ben might have had a girlfriend around here.'

That floored them for a bit. They looked at each other, then back at Charlie.

'It had never occurred to us,' admitted Katy. 'What you're meaning is that when he said he was going to the pub, he was really going to her, right?'

'Makes sense, doesn't it? Or maybe a bit of both. He seems to have . . . spent his life with ladies around him.'

'You don't have to pussyfoot around about it, you know,' said Alan.

'I suppose it does make sense,' admitted Katy. 'I don't suppose he even liked my mother very much, but they . . .'

'Did he ever say what pub he was going to?'

'No,' said Alan. 'But he never took the car.'

'What does that give us? The Portland Arms – that's a pretty rough joint.'

'That wouldn't worry Ben,' said Alan proudly. 'He wouldn't have set up this place if he was scared of rough types.'

'True. But he may have found the Portland a bit too much of a home from home. Then there's the Ale Machine and the Dodo. Those would be the only ones within easy walking distance of here, wouldn't they?'

'I suppose so,' said Alan. 'I'm not into pubs.'

It was said with a touch of the priggishness of the young – that same priggishness, maybe, that had made him and Katy such enthusiastic workers at the refuge. They obviously wanted to get back to what they were going to tell Ben when they visited him in hospital, so Charlie left them to it.

The nearest pub was the Portland Arms, and it showed every sign of being a rough pub: the stuffing was coming out of several of the seats, one window was boarded up, the music was too loud, and the landlord had tattooed arms and a fag hanging out of his mouth. When Charlie, fearing a succession of pub sessions, ordered a fruit juice, he was treated like something out of *Star Trek*. In this environment anything but a pint of bitter needed justifying, so Charlie flicked his ID at the barman.

'Oh Gawd, what is it this time? Has Jimmy Bates been flogging things out the back yard? You lot know I can't keep an eye on what goes on out there. You can see how short-staffed I am –'

'It's the attempted murder,' said Charlie succinctly. Even in the vicinity of the Portland Arms attempted murder was a rarity.

'Oh aye, that. It's got people talking, has that.'

'Did he drink here?'

'Who? Him that was knifed? Not that I remember myself, but people were saying last night that he come in here once or twice when he first bought the house. Mike, wasn't it you as said he'd been in?'

Mike shambled over, a beer belly clutching a pint mug.

'Who?'

'Chap who's been knifed.'

'Who wants to know?' Charlie flicked his ID again, knowing it would result in customer-resistance. 'Sure, I never would have come over if I'd known. I don't have nothin' to do with the police if I can help it. Show them an Irish accent an' they arrest it.'

'I'm arresting nobody,' said Charlie, peaceably. 'All I want to know is where he drinks – if he did.'

'He came in here once. Had a pint, sat watching, then went out an' I never saw him again.'

'Why did you notice him?'

Mike took a deep swig.

'First of all because he stood out, an' then because the rumour went around that he was opening a house for dossers. He stood out because he was middle class. He may have worked with roughs and dossers, but he wasn't a rough himself. Try the Dodo – they'd be more his type there.'

He shambled away, and Charlie decided that, though the manner was unpolished, the advice was good.

The Dodo was a different place altogether. There was evidence of a brisk lunchtime trade, the music was quiet and middle-of-the-road, and several of the drinkers had collars and ties on. In some parts of Bramsey they stoned you if you were wearing a collar and tie. Charlie ventured on a half of keg bitter. When he presented his ID to the landlord the man's eyes became veiled, and he just stood there, waiting.

'It's about the double knife attack in Portland Terrace.'

'Oh aye.'

154

'I believe Ben Marchant was a regular here.'

He chanced his arm because he believed that the man would deny it if he could. The gamble paid off.

'Not to say regular. He's been in now and again.'

'How often? Once a week? Twice a week?'

'Difficult to say. A month or two ago it was quite regular: maybe twice, even three times a week. That sort of tailed off. I don't think we'd seen him in the last ten days.'

'I see. Did he have any friends here? Drinking partners? Girlfriends?'

The landlord shifted uneasily.

'Look, mate, we don't like talking about our customers here. They've got a right to their privacy. It's bad enough him getting knifed like that. I don't want this pub to get a bad name like the Portland.'

'Look,' said Charlie reasonably, 'I'm investigating an attempted murder. Finding who did it takes precedence over your good name, right? Do you want me to go round asking all your customers?'

'No, no. Don't do that.'

'Then answer my question. The man's at death's door. He doesn't have any secrets at the moment.'

The landlord shifted on his feet.

'It wasn't him I was worried about. She's a regular, and a nice woman, and I don't want to land her in it.'

'What's her name?'

'Bessie ... Oh, what's her surname? Godber, that's it. Social worker. Black. Moved here about a year ago. Nice lady. Popular. Does a lot of good.'

'And he and she met up here?'

'Far as I know. I'm not the gossip columnist of the *Bramsey Times*. They began sitting together when they were here – laughing, chatting, going off together. No harm in that.'

'Did I say there was?'

'I'd've said it was a happy, harmless affair – not too serious. And Bessie most certainly isn't a crazy knife-wielder.'

'Would you know where Bessie lives?'

'Well, I didn't, but they were all talking in here earlier on.

It seems she lives on the Wellcome Estate – those big blocks down Mitching Lane. Don't know which one.'

'Did you say she was a social worker?'

'That's right.'

'Then she's really living on the job, isn't she?'

Oddie found the lottery company very hard work indeed. They went on about confidentiality, their clients' trust, their responsibilities under the Act – almost as if they were a top Lincoln's Inn law firm, or even a Swiss bank. The fact that it was the police asking made them marginally more respectful than if it was a tabloid reporter, but it didn't make them more unbuttoned. Quite early on Oddie lost hope of getting the size of Ben Marchant's win out of them, and he tried to pin them down instead on whether he had had a win at all.

'If we told you he'd had a win,' said the voice, obviously experienced in fending off the curious, 'even if we didn't tell you the sum, it would still be a breach of our undertaking to our client.'

'Client' affected Oddie very much as being called a 'customer' by British Rail did: they were small-time gamblers, for Christ's sake. But he managed to keep his temper, and keep the sweet reasonableness in his voice.

'The fact is', he said, not entirely truthfully, 'that we are pretty sure this man is not a client of yours at all. He seems to have used the lottery to explain a large sum of money which in fact he came by . . . let's just say by illegal means. That would reflect badly on the lottery . . .'

It took another ten minutes, and a scarcely veiled threat to get his chief constable to approach the Home Secretary (a man pathetically anxious to get a reputation for being tough on crime – indeed for being tough on anything) about lottery confidentiality as a shield for the criminal, before they would consent to put Ben Marchant's name through their computer. When they had done so they came back to him and, in the voice of an Irish bishop talking about his sex life to a Sunday newspaperman, said: 'No win of any kind at all.'

*   *   *

156

When he got to the Wellcome Estate, Charlie decided that the best way to find out where in the tatty beehive Bessie Godber lived was to ask one of her likely charges. He picked on a skinny, harassed-looking young mother wheeling a pram with one hand and leading a toddler with the other. She seemed glad to talk to anyone adult, and pointed to one of the blocks.

'She's in Grimshaw, seventh floor. But I think she's away. I was round there yesterday afternoon, and there was a note on the door.'

'I'll give it a go,' said Charlie.

The lift smelt of urine, and Charlie decided to use the stairs. The stairs smelt of urine too. What impulse led people to micturate communally, he wondered? Or was it perhaps children locked out of their flats while their mothers were at work? He ran up, taking breaths sparingly.

On the seventh floor he looked around for a door with a note on. It was at the far end of the landing. The note, which the girl he'd talked to presumably couldn't read, said: 'Away at a conference. Back Thursday afternoon.' It was then Thursday afternoon. The landing was bleak and bare, but the cold stone floor was clean. It was lit by windows at both ends. Charlie lingered, unwilling to waste a seven-floor run. From the window just by the flat he looked down on a meagre concrete play area, then on to scraps of green beyond, and beyond that on street upon street of red-brick terraced houses. From the other he looked down on the entrance to Grimshaw block, and here he struck lucky. A taxi was drawing up, and from it an ample black woman was emerging, paying the driver and collecting a suitcase from the boot. Charlie waited.

She didn't see him when she emerged from the lift, but Charlie could see her. Vital, genial, tough was how he summed her up. She strode along to her door, tore the note off it, then inserted her key in the door.

'Miss Godber?' said Charlie, coming up behind her.

'Mrs Godber, or Bessie,' she said, turning round. 'What can I do for you, young man?'

157

Charlie pulled out his ID, and she inspected it with an experienced eye.

'Well, well. Where you from, young man?'

'Brixton.'

'Where you from before that?'

'Brixton.'

She grinned, acknowledging his refusal to start off on a footing of any shared island background.

'Have it your own way. I'm just not used to black coppers. Bet you get a lot of aggro.'

'No more than you, I should think.'

She grinned agreement, and shrugged.

'Water off a duck's back.'

She led the way into a large, light, well-furnished flat. It was more than comfortable, it was smart.

'My penthouse apartment,' she said, with pride in her voice. She took from the hall table a notice that said PLEASE RESPECT MY PRIVACY OUTSIDE WORKING HOURS and stuck it on her front door. Inside the living room they both sat down and resumed the conversation where it had left off.

'They accept me now. I was an oddity at first – Bramsey's not a black area, as I'm sure you know. That was one reason why I wanted to take the job. I didn't want to be pigeonholed as a "black problems" person.'

'I know the feeling.'

'Which of my charges is in trouble this time?'

'None are, far as I know. None that I'm dealing with, anyway. This is to do with your private life.'

'Don't have no private life to speak of,' she grinned. 'First my daughter got married, then my son moved to Manchester. I love them and they love me, but our lives have separated now. That's why I was happy to move here.'

'Seems a bit like living on a powder keg to me.'

'Mostly they respect my private life. If they don't, I give them hell. West Indians are martyrs to bricks and mortar, boy.'

'Eh?'

'We say "I'm not paying rent to no council or landlord". So we buy a house, and it has to be cheap, and that means it's old and falling down, and when something needs doing, which it does all the time, we find someone who'll fix it cheap, and then it needs fixing again six months later. When I got this job I said to the council: "I want a flat, and I want a big one, because it'll be my office too." So now the council fixes things that go wrong, if I come on real strong at them, which I do, and I make it nice here and spend all my spare money on myself. In my work time I'm caring and compassionate and help people with their problems. In my own time I'm a selfish woman who pampers herself and likes a bit of luxury.' She pulled herself up and peered accusingly at Charlie. '*What* private life, young man?'

'The private life you want your charges to respect, I suppose,' he said cheekily. 'Ben Marchant.'

'Oh, *that* private life.'

She said it dismissively, as if it wasn't important to her. She obviously had not heard the news, away at her conference.

'Ben's been attacked. He's badly hurt, not out of danger yet.'

This time she did react, open-mouthed.

'Oh God! Poor Ben! One of his dossers, was it?'

Charlie was interested that she and Lady Mallaby shared the same assumption.

'Maybe, maybe not,' he said. 'Why do you think that?'

'He's got some pretty hopeless specimens there, I'd guess.'

'Was it his setting up the refuge brought you together?'

She shook her head vigorously.

'Not at all. I have practically nothing to do with the homeless.'

'Really?'

'Really. They've fallen through the net, and they accept the fact.' She leaned forward, self-justifying. 'Look, you in the police don't go out looking for dead bodies on the off-chance, do you? You investigate when one's brought to your notice. I don't go out canvassing dossers and trying to help them. I wait for them to come to me. And mostly they don't.'

'So you're not sympathetic?'

'I'm *very* sympathetic. They've had the rawest of raw deals from life. And all they get from politicians is empty words at best, hostility at worst. Very soon they're going to rediscover the Elizabethan idea of the "sturdy beggar", and Conservative politicians are going to demand they be whipped.'

'And Labour politicians are going to demand they be whipped even harder,' said Charlie, who was nothing if not politically impartial. Bessie Godber threw back her head and laughed. Then she got back to justifying herself.

'But my work takes up all my stock of sympathy and love and compassion. I know what Ben's doing, but he doesn't bring *his* stock of sympathy and compassion here. We never talk about it.'

'What brought you together?'

'Sex. A young man like you shouldn't need to ask.'

'That's all?'

'Well, I wouldn't be interested if I didn't like the man. We met up at the Dodo and the spark lit between us, you know? Ben's a charmer. He's so used to it that he takes it for granted, but you take my word for it – he knows it.'

'He's had a long line of woman friends.'

'I know. He talks about some of them.'

'Did he talk about his lottery win too?'

'Oh yes.'

'Did he tell you how much?'

'No. Probably thought it would bring out the gold-digger in me!'

'Did you believe him, about the lottery?'

She frowned.

'Funnily enough, something inside me didn't. I don't know why. Plenty of people are having lottery wins, no reason why Ben shouldn't. But it all seemed so convenient, everything came too pat. Winning a lottery so you could set up a home for the homeless, somehow it didn't ring true. I think I could have believed it more easily if he'd splurged it on big cars and fast living.'

'What other explanation is there?'

She shrugged.

'Not my business. If I started investigating all the lies I'm told I'd never get a hand's turn of real work done. Maybe he got it off that lady out at Otley. Ben could charm birds from trees.'

'If it was given him as a philanthropic gesture, it's difficult to see why it should be kept quiet.'

'If it was that, maybe that's what she wanted. You broadcast gestures like that and you get the whole world on your back. You must know that: send a small cheque to Save the Whale and you get Oxfam, Save the Children and the RSPB bombarding you with junk-mail appeals.'

'He told the lottery story to me, too.'

'So what? Is it obligatory to trust the police these days? They blabber as much as anyone else. If a TV personality's being questioned, or Linford Christie, some publicity hound in blue rushes straight out and tells the media. Get real.'

'I take your point . . . Do you love Ben?'

'No.'

'Do you trust him?'

She took some time to consider.

'No. Not entirely. He's left a long line of broken hearts, from what he's told me. You can say he's honest about it, tells everyone he's not made for faithfulness, but in the end the woman's likely to get drawn in, and in the end it's her who's left bruised and lonely, while Ben escapes Houdini-like from his chains and his box on the riverbed, and in one bound he's free and ready to start out all over again with someone else.'

'But you won't be hurt when – if – he moves on.'

'I know the type. I'm a social worker. I know all the types, believe me, particularly the unreliable ones. But in the end Ben was bound to go one step too far, bound to meet some woman who wouldn't accept it when he moved on.'

'It's possible he just has,' said Charlie.

CHAPTER 17

Straws in the Wind

The man on the bed was a face only. Below that he was bandages, and a shape under the bedclothes, but they had left a hand out, with a piece of board to tap on. The face looked a little drowsy, but Oddie and Charlie, as they approached and sat down, still could find traces of the man's intelligence – even of the old charm. Oddie, seeing him for the first time, caught a faint flash of the Pied Piper appeal.

'Hello, Mr Marchant,' he said. 'I believe you know D C Peace. He's on the case with me. We're going to ask you a few questions, and if you'd just tap once if the answer is yes, twice if the answer is no – right?' The eyes seemed to want to ask something, and Oddie hastily added: 'If you can't answer, don't tap at all. Is that understood?'

One tap.

'Do you remember what happened on Tuesday night?'

One tap.

'You were in the dining room with Mehjabean Haldalwa. Did someone come into the room?'

One tap.

'Did you see that person?'

Two taps.

'Did you see anything at all of him or her – hair, an item of clothing, maybe shoes?'

Two taps.

'Did you get any impression? Did you, for example, think it was a man or a woman?'

Pause, then one tap.

'Was the impression that it was a woman?'

Two taps.

'A man, then. He slashed Mehjabean, then slashed you. He wanted to injure *both* of you, then. Do you have any idea who would have wanted to hurt both you and her?'

Two taps.

'Would Mehjabean's father, for example?'

Two taps.

'Are you conscious of having enemies?'

Two taps.

'No one you've injured?'

Two taps. Oddie repressed a feeling of irritation.

'I think that's all I need to ask you.'

The eyes beneath the bedrail closed. They took themselves out into the corridor, then spoke in hushed tones.

'Is he saying nothing because he's got nothing to say, or is he saying nothing because he's shielding someone?' Oddie asked.

'I don't know,' said Charlie thoughtfully. 'But somehow I feel he knows something, or has guessed something, which he's not willing to pass on.'

'I feel the same.'

'Mind you, judging him in his present condition is hardly fair. Usually you've got body language and suchlike to help you form an opinion. With him at the moment you haven't even got face language. He hardly moved a muscle.'

'Added to which he was very drowsy, and probably not thinking straight. But the question arises: if he is shielding someone, who could it be? He would hardly shield his attacker, would he? Or could he be doing it for the Haldalwa girl?'

'You don't think she could have done it?'

'No, not really. I don't see any tendency towards self-inflicted wounds *there*, particularly potentially disfiguring ones. But what if it was someone close to her, and he thought the best thing was not to tell us?'

'Bloody fool if he thought that.'

'I asked him questions about her father to see what sort of reply I got. Notice that he replied with answers that he couldn't possibly have known – that Haldalwa would not want to hurt both him and Mehjabean and so on.'

'He just tapped. It was just an opinion,' Charlie pointed out.

'If he is shielding them, it would give him a handle on the family. Has it ever occurred to you that Ben Marchant rather likes playing God?'

'Yes, it has,' said Charlie frankly. 'Even – judging him harshly – that he's a spider-God, spinning benevolent-seeming webs. You could say that Alan and Katy have been caught in one. It's a point of view, a possibility. What are you going to do now?'

'I just want a word with the doctors. See when, if ever, we'll be able to have a real talk with him. Looking at him, I'm not hopeful.'

'Mind if I go and talk to Mehjabean? She had them phone me from the hospital that she was going home – back to the Centre – and would like to talk to me.'

'Fine. You go along. You may get more joy out of her than I would, or both of us together.'

Mehjabean was a much more lively figure to contemplate than Ben, sitting up in Katy's bed, *Wuthering Heights* open against her knees, a box of sweets near her right hand. Her liveliness of mind and temperament triumphed over the plaster covering her right cheek, and when she heard Charlie's 'Hello, Midge' she looked up to see him towering over her, and would have grinned broadly if it hadn't been painful.

'Hello, Charlie.'

'How do you know my name?'

'Seems you're pretty well known at the hospital. Seems both victims and criminals often land up there.'

'They do. Some of them have to be chained to their beds. One tried to take the bed with him once.'

'But I gather Charlie is a nickname – after some criminal or other.'

'Policeman-killer, middle of the last century. It was more of a big deal then. I'll tell you my real name one day, if you promise not to laugh. Now – you wanted to talk to me.'

'Yes,' said Midge slowly. She had been putting off the

moment. 'I'm afraid it's really nothing – maybe even pure imagination. It's just that Alan said I ought to try to remember, that maybe some little thing would come back that was crucial. I thought he was being a bit Hercule Poirot, and I tell you it really is *painful* to remember back – not just my own pain, but cradling Ben in my lap and all that . . . But what brought back a memory, or seemed to, was the words Alan used, because he said "something light as a feather", and it brought back this memory – if it *is* a mem –'

'Yes?'

'Sorry, I'm rambling, aren't I? Just before it happened – a second, half a second before – I felt on my face, my cheek, the other one, a sort of light, tickling feeling, like a feather might make, and *then* –' she flinched.

'Then you felt the knife?'

'Yes. I can hardly bear to think about it.'

'Then don't. But – let's say it wasn't actually a feather – could you make a guess at what it might be?'

'No. I've thought and thought. I nearly didn't call you because it sounds so silly, not knowing what it could be. What could give a feeling so *light*. Charlie – bend down.'

'Eh?'

'Bend down. I pulled this feather out of my pillow – just like Cathy in *Wuthering Heights*. Shut your eyes. *This* is what it felt like.' She gently drew the feather across his cheek. 'Just for a moment. And then there was the pain.'

Next morning it was tying up loose ends time. Or rather, pursuing loose strands that could be nothing, could be significant. Every interesting case had many of these, because every case involved willy-nilly people whose lives had suddenly been intersected by crime, and a conscientious policeman had to find out whether this was by chance or by design.

They had a large Trades Directory at police headquarters, and it was brief and factual on Sabre plc. Its head office was in SW1, but its factory and a subsidiary office was in Leeds. Interesting, Charlie thought. But a check with the police computer drew a total blank, as did a check on Sir George Mallaby, beyond the fact that he had tested positive when breathalysed in 1990, but only marginally over the limit, so he had escaped with a warning. A blameless life. Or should there be a question mark after that, Charlie wondered.

It might be worth paying a visit, he decided, to the *Yorkshire Post* offices in Wellington Street. He knew a friendly young lady in the archives section, who would always turn up whatever had got into print on whatever or whoever was interesting him at the moment. He phoned her first, went through the ritual chatting-up that was part of their relationship, then told her what he wanted. When he arrived they grinned with the intimacy of people who would have fancied each other if not already attached – or, truth to tell, *did* fancy each other, regardless – and then she shook her head and pointed to a pile of papers.

'The records hardly come up trumps,' she said. 'Company reports, Annual General Meetings, a couple of rounds of redundancies, but minor ones. What there is there, you're welcome to, and it's all there.'

It was indeed a meagre haul. All together the pieces gave a picture of a middle-sized company, struggling during the long recession to retain a middling degree of profitability. It formed a convincing basis for Sir George's country land-owner status, while never suggesting he was going to be one of the country's leading tycoons.

Charlie was just closing the earliest of the papers, a *Yorkshire Evening Post* for April 1990, when his eye was caught by a picture, or rather a face in a picture. It showed a group at a Conservative function in one of the more marginal Tory constituencies in Leeds, attended by a government minister now discredited, and not particularly credited even then. He was, Charlie knew, one of the men who had escaped with extensive moral bruising in the arms for Iraq investigation. But that wasn't what interested Charlie. What had caught his eye was a woman to the side of the group, with immaculate hair-do, clothes that were certainly designed-label and probably Parisian, a confident social poise and – yes – beauty. Beauty of a certain age, but undoubtedly the real thing.

*   *   *

The knot of lunchtime locals in the Black Heifer in Monkton was not being co-operative. Oddie was used to that. He had left Charlie behind at the other, unpromising local toping house because a black detective was unlikely to prove helpful in the Heifer. He knew this and Charlie knew this, but it had not been mentioned. They were by now too close to need to touch on such topics. However, even without Charlie the going was tough. Most of the locals tended to back off to a distance and stick to it, while Oddie was left with a congenitally cussed old rustic.

'Marchant was well known around here, I suppose?'

'Aye.'

'A very good estate manager, Sir George said.'

''Appen.'

'You didn't think so?'

'I didn't say nowt to the contrary.'

'Bit of a one for the ladies, I heard.'

'Did you? . . .' Then in a burst of pseudo-informativeness: 'Us wouldn't know about that. Us be drinkers, not fornicators.'

There was an appreciative snicker all round.

'I'm sure you made a wise choice,' said Oddie, feeling like a sucker-up. 'Fornication doesn't seem to have done Ben Marchant much good, does it?'

There was no more than a complacent nodding of heads.

'I heard tell about him and a local postmistress – what was her name?'

They stared back at him.

'Post office's down the road. Name's over t'door,' said his informant.

'And a woman who owns a hat shop in Otley?' hazarded Oddie.

'Oh aye? . . . Not many hat shops around for the women-folk these days. They stand out. Shouldn't be difficult to find, if you have the nose.'

Oddie made an unwise last throw.

'And there was talk of one of the tenant farmer's wives.'

'Was there now? An' what if 'er 'usband was drinkin' 'ere

this day? 'Appen you'd be lookin' for a clout round the chops.'

Oddie drank the rest of his pint in silence.

The drinkery where Oddie had left Charlie was hardly more than a cottage – was attached, indeed, to a terrace of cottages, and was just a little higher, broader and deeper than they were. It was called the Farmer's Arms, and Charlie, once he had stooped to enter the public bar, found it poky, dimly lit, and probably dirty. Five or six pairs of eyes glinted in the gloom. Charlie had already decided that matiness was likely to get him nowhere.

'Pint of Tetley's,' he ordered, then looked around him. 'I expect you can guess who I am.'

'Oh aye,' came one reply, after a pause. It was not exactly hostile, more suspicious, defensive, emphasizing that they recognized he was different from them, because he was black, a cockney townie, and, above all, represented the law.

'Pints all round,' said Charlie. 'And there'll be a second where that came from.'

The fact that he did not make the second round conditional was immediately appreciated. There were gratified murmurs, drainings of glasses and trips to the bar.

'Now you're talking,' said one.

'And I hope you will be, too,' said Charlie.

'Well, we know what you want,' said one of them, a tall, gnarled grey-headed chap, who everyone seemed to look to. ''Twas you were out at t'Manor yesterday, warn't it?'

'Yes,' said Charlie. 'With my boss.'

'Boss gone on to t'Heifer, most like?' said the man acutely. Charlie nodded. ''E won't get nowt thee-ar.'

'Oh? Why not?'

'Gaffers' pub. Gaffers stick together.'

'And this is for the workers?'

'Aye, that's reet. You've got a head on thee, lad, even if thee is from town, and looks like thee's come out of t'chimney.'

General throaty, cigarette-coated chuckles.

'Ask away,' said someone. It was as near as dammit to a welcome.

'Was Marchant liked around here?' Charlie began with. There was a pause for consideration.

'Aye, as a bloke,' said his first informant, looking around to get a general confirmation. 'No quarrel wi' him as a bloke.'

'As the estate manager?'

'Middlin'. If 'e'd done all 'e promised, 'e'd've been the best estate manager ever. Only 'e didn't.'

'Like as not that were Sir George's doin',' hazarded one man.

'An' more likely still Sir George never 'eard 'alf o' what was promised, because it were forgotten as soon as the words were out o' his mouth,' said his main informant, who obviously prided himself on his plain talking. 'Fine talk, that were Ben Marchant's line. Only often as not it were never followed up.'

'What about his love life?'

'Oh, is that what you call it down in t'big city? 'Appen we should start talkin' o' the love life o' our cattle.'

'He was a stud bull, you mean?'

'Noo-oo,' said the old man judiciously, again looking round at his mates. 'Fair's fair. But 'e loved 'em an' left 'em.'

'I heard talk about someone who owned a hat shop.'

'Oh aye. Mrs Gregson. Husband works at the D S S in Leeds. Well out of the way all day. Not many customers for hats these days. Just put up the "Back in 'alf an hour" sign and you're away.'

'How long ago was this?'

'Matter o' two, three year ago.'

'And the local postmistress?'

'Sally. Aye, Sally's been reet lonesome since 'er 'usband passed on. Ben were a bit of a godsend to 'er.'

'Angry when it was broken off?'

The man shrugged.

'Who can tell? Not so's you'd notice. 'Urt, more like, I'd've said. Any road, it were four yee-ar sin' that they were goin' together. You don't rush out an' carve a bloke up four yee-ar after 'e's ditched you for someone else.'

'Who did he ditch her for?'

'Hattie Jenkins. Bob Jenkins is one of Sir George's tenants. Nice bloke – a bit dozy-like. Never caught on what were in the air. But it were never reet serious, that one. Just a bit o' fun now and again, when Bob were safely out on 'is tractor on one o' the far fields.'

'He could have found out recently.'

'Bob'd just 'ave scratched 'is ear and said, "Oh aye." There's nowt worries our Bob.'

'All this seems to be some time ago,' said Charlie, bringing out something that had been worrying him for a while.

'Ancient news,' agreed the worthy.

'Ben Marchant doesn't seem like the type to go in for celibacy all of a sudden.'

There was a chuckle, and several invaded the bar for their second pints.

'Seems to me we've been fed a lot of stale gossip,' said Charlie looking around. He met some reserved grins.

''Appen,' said his informant. 'And 'appen you're on the wrong scent entirely.'

'It's been known.'

'Mind you – us knows nothing.'

'There's knowing and knowing,' said Charlie. There were several nods and winks.

'Aye, there is. Us just suspects. Problem is, we're all employed by Sir George, either on 'is farm, or on one of the tenant farms.'

'He didn't strike me as an unfair man.'

'Oh, you sit talkin' to 'im for 'alf an hour and think you know your man, do you? Folk from London think they know it all, an' they know *nowt*. Point I'm makin' is: one o' us tells you the gossip that went round, 'e'd want it made worth 'is while.'

'I thought I had.'

'What, risk the sack for a couple o' pints o' Tetley's? You're wet behind the ears, young feller, for all you think you're smart . . . Now, for a double whisky an' a little jug o' warm water I'll tell you the talk that's been goin' around.'

Charlie sighed, raised his eyebrows towards the grimy ceiling, and turned to the bar. The farmworker turned to his fellows and winked. Everyone in the room save Charlie knew that old Harry would turn sixty-five come Friday, and would then leave Sir George's employ.

CHAPTER 18

The One Who Cared

It was three days before Charlie and Oddie took the road out to Otley again. There was so much to be looked into, so many connections to make. Rumour was not evidence; beguiling conjunctures of timings were possibilities, maybe even probabilities, but only by sightings or other concrete physical evidence could they be hardened into certainties. Some cases presented police detectives with massive, unavoidable definites; others dangled before them an infinite number of suggestive and tantalizing indefinites, and challenged them to form them into a pattern.

Once again they had phoned the Manor in advance to say that they were coming. 'Just a few small matters that needed to be tied up,' Oddie had said, in his comfortable Yorkshire voice. When they got to the gate and stated their business they got a cheery: 'Right-ho – you know the way.' They were let in by an amiable but mute Filipino, and in the drawing room they had a sense of seeing an early fifties comedy for the second time. Lady Mallaby was in another of her shapeless gardening garments, and Sir George was doing the country squire for all it was worth – firm handshake, fingering of the moustache, and offering of drinks with an off-hand recognition that they were on duty. The script could have been by William Douglas-Home.

'Sorry to get you in from your gardening,' said Oddie to Lady Mallaby, as they let Sir George pour them small sherries. 'Early evening's the nicest time for it, I always think.'

'Don't mention it,' she said, coming up to stand beside him at the French windows. 'I'd be coming in anyway to change and have a sherry before dinner. With a bit of luck you'll stay for a second one and I can eat dinner without changing. I like early evening too. You must have very little time for gardening in your job, though.'

'Very little, but I enjoy it when I can get out and help the wife. The *Colutea floribunda* doesn't seem to like it out here. Is the soil too clayey?'

'Much too,' said Lady Mallaby. 'It was a mistake even trying to grow it. I'll have it out and put an azalea there. Nothing sadder than straggly bushes, is there?'

She led the way back to the sofa, and they all sat down.

'I've had a talk with Ben Marchant since I saw you both,' said Oddie.

'Oh, Ben can talk now, can he?' said Sir George. 'On the mend – that's capital!'

'*I* talked. Mr Marchant just tapped his replies,' amended Oddie. 'Not a satisfactory form of interview, I'm afraid. But it does seem that he and the girl – her name is Mehjabean Haldalwa – saw nothing. Or at least, if he saw anything, he's saying nothing.'

'He would hardly keep quiet if he had anything to offer, would he?' volunteered Sir George. 'If the man's not caught, Ben will never be able to feel safe again.'

'So you'd have thought,' agreed Oddie neutrally, intent on keeping the temperature low. 'Unless he had some reason for keeping shtoom that outweighed the danger.'

'Difficult to imagine what that might be,' commented Lady Mallaby, her tone as bland as Oddie's.

'It is, yes. But we have advanced a step or two in a direction that could explain his caginess. We've established, for example, that he never had a National Lottery win.'

'What!' exclaimed Sir George.

'No, no biggish sum from Camelot, I'm afraid.'

'But – I mean, he was so *convincing*! –'

Oddie raised his eyebrows ironically.

'I think Ben Marchant has spent his life being convincing,' he said drily. 'So the question arises, where had he got the money to set up the refuge, and where did he get the money to run it week by week?'

'Some rich relative pegged out?' hazarded Sir George.

'Did he give the impression of coming from a moneyed background?'

'Not something you can always tell.'

'In any case, why would he lie, if that was the source? If he disapproved of inheriting money – and I've no earthly reason for thinking he might – is he likely to approve of a lottery that hands out multiple millions? The likeliest reason for his keeping quiet about who attacked him is that he or she was involved in the financing of the refuge, and the means of getting the money out of them was dubious, or downright crooked.'

'Doesn't sound like Ben,' said Lady Mallaby. Oddie wasn't going to give the impression he accepted unquestioningly their version of Ben's character.

'Maybe, maybe not. Certainly I've no evidence at all of any criminal activities by Marchant in the past. He has no record. On the other hand . . .'

'Yes?'

'I have a strong sense of him as a slightly Walter Mitty-like mind, seized by whatever was the fantasy or the project of the moment. I can imagine such a person being quite ruthless about how he got the money to "make his dreams come true". If the project was clearly a good, a benevolent thing, then I think he could be willing to sail on the windy side of the law. Especially if he could present the process to himself as something the person he was screwing money out of thoroughly deserved.'

Charlie had got a bit tired of his superior's circumlocution.

'We're talking blackmail,' he said.

'Yes. Yes, I can see that,' said Sir George, nodding his head in Charlie's direction. 'Difficult though to see who Ben might blackmail, or what sort of a hold he could have over them.'

He looked up to see two pairs of eyes fixed on him, and began immediately to bluster.

'I say! This is outrageous! Ben and I were perfectly good friends. You've no cause whatever –'

'It is awfully unfair,' said Oddie quietly, with an air of agreeing with him entirely. 'But as soon as the idea of black-

174

mail came up – and it would have to be blackmail for something more than peanuts – then it did occur to us that probably the only rich man he knew was you, that you were also his employer, and that he lived in your vicinity and was therefore in a position to know something about you that he could use.'

'If *that's* all you've got to go on,' said Sir George aggressively, 'then I'd advise you to be very careful what you say or do. Very careful indeed. If you do anything to damage my business I'll have your guts for garters.'

'There was something that struck both of us as just a little bit odd when we talked to you first,' said Oddie, ignoring his bluster but turning for confirmation in Charlie's direction. 'When we were talking about your business, Sabre plc, you said, "Ben had nothing to do with that".'

'Well, he didn't.'

'You may have a low opinion of policemen, Sir George – I know you've been a magistrate, and many magistrates do – but I assure you neither of us would have imagined that your estate manager out here was likely to have anything to do with the running of a heavy industry firm like Sabre plc.'

'Mountain out of a molehill,' said Sir George. 'Just trying to make the position clear.'

'It occurred to us, too, later, that you never actually told us what Sabre plc made. No reason why you should, of course, but it was just possible the omission was significant.'

'We make armaments.'

'Exactly. Not difficult to find that out. And we found out too that there have been rumours over the years – '

'I tell you, I'll – '

' – rumours about arms to Iraq and Iran. Recently rumours about arms to Nigeria.'

'If you damage my business or my reputation by spreading rumours which have no basis in fact, I'll go as high as need be to get you drummed out of the police.'

'Well, I wouldn't go as high as a government minister, if that's what you mean. They've tended to be broken reeds as far as armaments manufacturers are concerned –

encouraging them to slide round the regulations, then washing their hands as soon as they land in trouble. But we're talking here about rumours *already* in circulation, and in any case we're not primarily interested at the moment in possible breaches of international embargoes.'

'Then what the hell did you bring it up for?'

'What we're interested in is whether the money for the refuge came from you, and whether there was blackmail. The possible reasons for the blackmail we can go into at our leisure.'

'There was no blackmail. He had no cause to blackmail me.'

'Yet he had been continuing to come out here, hadn't he? Regularly – once a week, the locals say. Every Monday afternoon he'd be out here for an hour or two.'

Sir George changed tack.

'We took an interest in the Centre. Naturally. Ben had worked for us for many years. We were in on the project from the launching-pad stage. We're not a bleeding-hearts club in this house, but you can't help noticing all the young people on the streets. We hoped he'd make a go of his hostel.'

'So he reported out here on the progress once a week?'

Sir George spluttered.

'Yes. Yes, he did.'

'I suggest you contributed to its expenses.'

'Small sums. Occasionally.'

'Really? And yet he came here regularly as clockwork. On a Monday.' Oddie looked at Charlie, then smiled bleakly and spread out his hands. 'I think we should come clean with you, Sir George, Lady Mallaby. We think you've been putting on a charade for our benefit. There is Sir George, the bluff country squire with business interests, and there is his lady, the dumpy, frumpy wife whose great pleasure is working in her garden, because you can't get the staff these days. Sir George's role is one he's playing all the time out here at Otley. Yours, Lady Mallaby, was I suggest assumed for the occasion. When I mentioned *Colutea floribunda* you didn't catch on that it was a nonsense name I'd made up.'

'I never know the Latin names of plants. I could see the shrub you were looking at.'

'And what shrub was it, in popular language?'

'A . . . a jasmine.'

'Actually a daphne. You're no more a keen gardener than Sir George is a country squire.'

In the silence that followed Charlie put in his oar, looking hard at Susan Mallaby.

'I saw a picture of you the other day – a picture of you a few years ago at a Tory Party function,' he said. 'The real you is smart, still quite trim, and *very* good-looking. Anyone could have told us that, just as anyone who works at Sabre plc could have told us that Sir George is tough, foul-mouthed and a slave-driver of his work force – an industrialist with the necessary eye on the main chance. So the fact is, you were both in collusion on this, both playing parts for our benefit. What we want to know is why, and how did it come about?'

'That's it,' chimed in Oddie. 'We asked ourselves how this partnership – whether reluctant or enthusiastic – to put on a play for our benefit came about. Why was it necessary? And we note that Ben always came out here on a Monday, at a time when Sir George would almost certainly be at the Sabre works, and we note that the names of Ben's lady friends that you gave us related to affairs of his that were some years in the past.'

'And we noted another thing,' took up Charlie. 'Which is that Ben Marchant always seemed to take up with women decidedly older than himself. You yourself told us, Lady Mallaby, that one of his girlfriends was past child-bearing age. The mothers of both his children we know about – young people who are working at the Centre at the moment – are well into middle age. Ben himself, we have discovered, is just turned forty. He went for older women.'

'Why that should be isn't for us to ask,' said Oddie. 'Whether he preferred a woman with a lot of experience, whether he likes the fuller figure, whether he wanted gratitude. The plain fact is, that's what he preferred – prefers, I should say.'

177

'So it seemed logical, Lady Mallaby, to ask if the girlfriend he'd had out here since the last of the women whose names you gave us, might in fact have been you.'

Susan Mallaby remained silent, looking straight at them.

'You've no comment to make?' Oddie asked.

'None.'

'Very well,' he resumed. 'So the pattern that seemed to us to emerge is this. For some time Ben and you have been having an affair – whether or not with your husband's concurrence and blessing we don't know – and in the course of it, perhaps from pillow talk, perhaps because you were happy to give him a handle on your husband, Ben finds out from you that Sir George has been trading illegally in arms with countries that have been internationally declared to be beyond the pale.'

Again he looked at her. Still she looked back, unflinching and unspeaking.

'When Ben got the idea of the refuge – and Ben is a man of myriad ideas, which he pursues for a time, like his women, and then passes on to others – the question of money was vital. He had nothing, I would guess, beyond any saving he might have made from his salary here, and I don't get the feeling that Ben is a saving sort of person. So he began the process that I will call blackmailing, though no doubt he managed to present it in a much kindlier light: in return for his silence, you were providing initial help with the project, and then a small weekly sum as a contribution to its running expenses.'

'This is fucking preposterous,' said Sir George, his civility slipping badly. 'There were no illegal arms sales, so how could he blackmail me?'

'I think, you know, that we'll find out about the illegal arms sales once we start digging. I think it's important to realize that the sums involved in the blackmail, though sizeable, were not enormous. Those decrepit late-Victorian terrace houses go for comparatively little. To a reasonably successful businessman and country landowner they were affordable. Feeding nine or ten people a fairly basic meal each night wasn't vastly expensive. And Ben was far from a professional blackmailer. I don't imagine when you went along with this gentle pressurizing for funds that you foresaw it escalating in the usual blackmailer's way. It was much more in the nature of a quid pro quo: you know something I don't want known; I'm willing to pay you an agreed sum if you keep quiet about it.'

'Practically standard business practice,' commented Charlie. 'But someone has tried to kill him, and that's what we're *really* interested in.'

Oddie nodded.

'So if we can't see it in Ben to keep upping the ante – because we have no evidence he was interested in money for itself – we have to look for other possibilities. Did you, Sir George, only recently find out about Ben and your wife, and were you driven mad with jealousy? Possible in the abstract, but it hardly rings true to character or situation. Around here one person's business seems to be everyone's business. I think the important thing is that there is no sense of this being a *planned* murder attempt. No one could have gone to the refuge expecting to find Ben or Mehjabean alone, and to be able to kill or maim them without being recognized. The conclusion must be that it was a spur-of-the-moment affair, one born of an overmastering emotion, and botched for that very reason.'

'So what we need to look at,' said Charlie, 'is what happened that evening.'

'You know about the spot of bother at the Centre?' said Oddie.

'What bother? You told us nothing about that,' said Sir George, puffing self-importantly.

'Your wife knows. I'm sure she's told you. Let's look at the sequence of events. The proposed husband of Mehjabean, an Asian girl at the refuge, comes along, apparently to say that the arranged marriage between them is off. She has nothing to fear. The residents come to bar him from seeing her and preferably to see him off, very protective of the girl. While the row is going on, Mrs Ingram arrives, sees the row, is rather pleased for reasons of her own, *and recognizes Ben Marchant.*'

179

'We went over the fact that she knew him from before,' said Sir George.

'Yes, we did. The first thing that occurred to her was that if he was the man who had come into a big lottery win, as rumour had it, he should damned well support the handicapped child he'd had by her sister. When she got home, much later, she rang her family down in Lincolnshire and pressed this view strongly.'

'But before that,' said Charlie, 'she went to a Conservative Party recruitment do, of her own organizing. Rather a posh affair at the Royal, because she likes to do things in style and wanted to attract the right sort of person – very dainty nibbles and a carvery afterwards. This was a drive for the Leeds area as a whole, which includes Otley. Hardly any recruits, as it turned out, but lots of party stalwarts. And when she met Lady Mallaby there, it was another aspect of Ben Marchant's career that struck her.'

'Here we have to go carefully,' said Oddie. 'Because according to Mrs Ingram all she said to Lady Mallaby was, "I've just been round to that Centre place, run by your old estate manager. What a lot of trouble these do-gooders cause." Mrs Ingram is very anxious now to distance herself from the refuge, from Ben Marchant, and from any suggestions that she may have been a catalyst in an attempted murder.'

'But with Mrs Ingram it's always advisable to check her statements. We've talked to others who were nearby, and they tell us she said rather more than that,' said Charlie. 'Putting accounts together it seems that what she also said, roughly, was: "He's got some coloured girl he's interested in, and all hell is breaking out there with her family."'

Oddie looked closely at Lady Mallaby, but her eyes were unclouded with hate or rage.

' "Coloured" is the sort of word that's not used in politically correct circles these days,' said Oddie. 'But we're not talking about circles like that. Older people still use it all the time. It's all-purpose, and it covers a multitude of shades. And you'd heard the rumour, hadn't you, Lady Mallaby, that Ben was now going with a "coloured" woman?'

She stared ahead, still unflinching and silent.

'After that, people at the buffet dinner say you helped yourself to more food, hardly talked to anybody else, then abruptly put down your plate and left. Mrs Ingram no doubt saw this with amusement, because the only reason she'd said that was to annoy and upset you. She'd heard rumours. We're told the time you left was about half past nine. We've timed the drive to Portland Terrace. You would have got there around ten to ten – just the time.'

'You would have parked the car,' resumed Charlie, 'walked up to the house, and through the lighted window you would have seen facing you, backs to the hall door, Ben and Mehjabean – your lover and his "coloured" girlfriend, as you thought. Ben's hand was on her hand. A great wave of hatred swept over you. You'd been replaced by a beautiful young woman. At last Ben had in you what was surely inevitable in the long run – a lover who would not let him go, who would not be content with being just good friends, would not indulge him as a child is indulged. You saw them together, you ran into the house –'

'How did she get in?' demanded Sir George. 'Wasn't the front door locked?'

'It was. We guess that she'd got a key after Ben had bought the houses, and while he was setting up the refuge there. It was an obvious place to . . . meet. She stood for a moment in the open door of the dining room. Then she attacked.'

'What with?' came back Sir George. 'My wife isn't the sort of woman who carries a knife around with her.'

'She had just been to a buffet dinner, with a carvery. She had helped herself to unwanted food. That's when she took the knife.'

'Prove it.'

'The caterers say a knife is missing.'

'Prove my wife took it.'

'We hope to prove it by finding it here,' said Oddie, his voice confident. 'And bloodstained clothes. I have a warrant, and a team from Leeds will be on its way by now. I imagine you both of you know where they're hidden, don't you? When you got home you must have told your husband everything and you made your plans. You concocted the charade which you've played out for us, and you got rid of the evidence.'

'Why did your husband go along with it, we wonder?' asked Charlie. 'Was it because he still loves you? Was it because he was afraid of a trial for attempted murder harming his business? Or was it that he was afraid that once the police started digging into the background of it, the financing of the refuge must come out, and then the blackmail?'

'We don't really need to go into that yet,' said Oddie. 'We'll be investigating the illegal arms sales, so there may be charges there, as well as the charge of accomplice after the fact.'

'You're bloody jumping the gun, aren't you?' said Sir George, his face apoplectic.

'A little, perhaps. The important thing at the moment is finding the weapon, and maybe the bloody clothes, if they haven't been burnt. Not so easy, these days, to burn things, in houses that have oil or gas-fired central heating. Is there a hat with a feather among the clothes, I wonder? Or perhaps still in your wardrobe, Lady Mallaby? Mehjabean felt one against her cheek just before the knife attack. The cloakroom attendant at the Royal said you were wearing one when you arrived and left. We'll look for that, and the other things. We'll search the house from top to bottom, and then we'll search the grounds and the garden – look for earth that's been newly dug over –'

Lady Mallaby's eyes went down to her lap. Oddie knew that he had made a hit. He knew better than to say anything. The seconds ticked by. Then she raised her head.

'I've always believed in taking the consequences of what I have done. That's part of being a grown-up person. I should have stayed there, shouldn't I? But the instinct of self-preservation is very strong. I should have stayed there and said: "This is one woman he can't use. This is one woman he can't employ his spoilt-little-boy tactics on."' She looked at Oddie. 'The knife and the clothes are close to the laburnum tree. That's one thing in the garden I do know the name of.'

CHAPTER 19

Consequences

The Centre was abuzz with noise and activity when Charlie dropped in there three days later. The police had given the go-ahead for normal activity to be resumed. Residents whose fortnight was up and more than up were moving out. People had begun calling in the hope of securing the vacant rooms. Everyone was on the go, and the priority was the room that Mouse had vandalized. The extent of the damage ensured that it needed both an undercoat and a top coat. Fortunately there was a lot of paint left from the time when Ben had taken the houses over. They had found it in a coalshed at the back of number twenty-two, and Derek was organizing an emergency top-speed renovation job when Charlie came into the familiar back room and kitchen at twenty-four.

'You two go and slap on the undercoat,' he said to Katy and Mehjabean, beautiful under bandages. 'Thick as you like over the bits where the little scrote left his mark. Oh, I wish he'd come crawling back looking for a room! I'd accommodate him! When we do the top coat we may have to do two walls one colour, two another. Though we've got two shades of blue, so maybe we could do the bottom half dark, the top light. Anyway, it's not the Savoy . . .'

Katy and Midge went off together quite happily, rapt in each other's company, seemingly incurious about anything Charlie could tell them. They had been told someone had been arrested for the attack, the name meant nothing to them, and they were getting back without further thought to the routines of before the violence. Charlie wondered at the elasticity of the young, their ability to live in the present.

'Right,' he said to the other two. 'I guess you want me to be quick.'

'Please,' said Alan, looking at his watch. 'I've got the shopping to do, and then I said I might drop in on my mum and dad.'

'OK. Now, as you know, someone has been arrested for the attempted murder – Lady Mallaby, an old girlfriend – former girlfriend, that is – of Ben Marchant's. I've talked to Ben: he can talk a little now, but we had a very restricted time with him. He won't be part of the prosecution evidence, but she has confessed. We've got some forensic back-up – some soil deposits from the front room here, identifiable as from the Otley area. We think the charges will stick.'

'What about here? The refuge?' asked Alan.

'Yes – that's a more difficult matter, at least in the long term. Of course it's not any concern of ours, but obviously you need information about the background to this place. The money for it came from Lady Mallaby's husband. There may eventually be charges against him on quite another matter, but the investigation will take time, a long time. If he is charged, then there could be questions about how the money for the refuge was obtained.'

'Isn't that all a bit hypothetical?' Alan asked.

'Yes,' agreed Charlie. 'That's why I said the problems were long term. In the short term the refuge is safe enough. But Sir George was also contributing a weekly subsidy – for food, heating, lighting and so on. That will stop. The question is: can you keep going without it? You'll have to talk to Ben: he may have a nest-egg tucked away somewhere that will tide you over while he's recovering. If not –'

Alan's eyes and Derek's went to each other.

'We might charge for the evening meal,' Alan said dubiously. 'They do *have* money – from begging and that.'

'What about the do-gooding organizations?' asked Derek.

'I was going to suggest them,' said Charlie. 'Shelter's the best-known one. You could start with them. Go along and talk to someone there. There'll be lots of negative publicity to overcome, remember. Go on your own, Derek – sorry,

Alan, but you and Katy are too young to help the cause in an interview.'

'Course I wouldn't go,' said Alan scornfully. 'I'm not completely thick.'

'Sorry. Anyway, if they can't help you themselves they'll be able to give good advice. It'll then be a question of knocking on doors. I presume you're waiving the fortnightly rule as far as Derek is concerned?'

'Oh, that's all sorted out,' Alan said. 'Derek will be staying till Ben's fully fit again. He's taking over his room.'

'Good. Remember, the Centre has enemies all around, and not just Mrs Ingram. She's keeping very quiet about it, and rumour has it her political ambitions have been stalled. But no politician is the natural friend of a place like this, because none of their constituents want it in their neighbourhood. So be prepared. Derek will need to present a full account to funders of how the place is run, the rules and regulations, the weekly cost per person, and so on.'

'I'm halfway there already,' said Derek. 'I'll go over it in detail with Alan and Katy, try to have a few words with Ben. We'll sort something out.'

'We'll all go and see Ben tonight or tomorrow,' said Alan. 'Midge can come too. He's fond of her. Well, if that's all, I'd better be getting along.'

When he had gone, Charlie raised his eyebrows at Derek.

'Are they taking it quite as much in their stride as they seem to be?' he asked. Derek Redshaw shrugged.

'As far as I can see. Now that Ben is out of danger they seem mainly worried about whether they can keep this place going till he comes out.'

'Neither of them is talking about going back to live with their families?'

'No. They think the burden of the refuge is on their shoulders at the moment. Alan goes back now and again, and he seems to be getting on all right with them. But he says they don't understand.'

'Tell me something new.'

'I did hear that rather often from the kids on the streets.'

185

'On or off the streets, this and every previous generation. Start worrying when the parents do understand.'

'I wouldn't know about that. I was in care by the time I got to the rebellious stage.'

'What about Katy?'

'She's been back to see her mother. I suggested they just have an evening together, without getting into any heavy discussion.'

'Sounds like a sensible idea.'

'*Seems* to have worked out well enough. I think Katy is more able to set the agenda than before. Could be we might get her back home by the time school starts up again. Alan's talking about taking a year out. That wouldn't be too disastrous, would it?'

'No. Might do him good. What about Mehjabean?'

'They're taking it slowly, like she was advised by the lawyer. I get the feeling Moslem parents have the sort of authority that British ones did a hundred years ago.'

'I think you may be right. For better or worse. But I don't think Mr Haldalwa is a natural tyrant, or anything like that.'

'Anyway, she'll be going carefully, with legal advice. I'll go with her to the solicitor if anything unexpected comes up, though I think she's more capable of taking care of herself than I am.'

'Good. She may seem capable, but she needs an older shoulder. Can you drive?'

'Sure. The army taught me that. The army taught me lots, except how to survive in real life.'

'Well, I must be getting along,' said Charlie, getting up, and looking around possibly for the last time. 'I can be contacted at the police headquarters if you need me. Just one more thing: how do you think the kids view their father now?'

Derek looked up, rather bemused.

'They're very concerned about him, of course.'

'That wasn't what I meant. Deeper down, longer term.'

Derek frowned.

'I suppose you mean: is he a hero to them, a knight of the shining path, a redeemer come to change their whole lives?'

'Yes, roughly.'

'I don't think so. I don't mean they've seen through him, or that the glamour has worn off, or anything like that. But I think that already, before all this, the kids had begun to take him in their stride – just use the experience of working with him, knowing it would end, and they'd move on. That's how I interpret what they say about him. They're devoted to this place, they'll do anything for him, but they know it's not their life.'

'I hope so,' said Charlie. 'I really hope so.'

Because an idea had come to him when they were talking to Ben the previous day. He had expressed great concern about Alan and Katy, he had asked what was happening about Mehjabean, and he had expressed satisfaction that the refuge was still up and running, that someone was standing in for him. But once or twice during the interview Charlie had caught a faraway look in Ben's eyes, as if what they were talking about was already something in his past, and he was moving on to a new dream.

Act of Darkness

Simon Shaw

Philip Fletcher, not yet fully recovered from his latest bout of life-threatening misdemeanours, takes a recuperative, undemanding job at the Chichester Festival for the summer season. What could be more pleasant (he reasons) than to idle away a relaxing few months in the countryside at the scene of some of his greatest triumphs?

But Fletcher's rural idyll is disturbed by an undercurrent of sinister goings-on, and with two obsessive stalkers on the loose – not to mention that unspeakably loathsome and utterly untalented thespian, Richard Jones – there's once again a premium on his dubious criminal skills. And in the ominous quiet of the Sussex countryside, the hunter soon becomes the hunted . . .

'As usual, the behind-the-scenes banter of artistic egos is conveyed with wit and elegance'

MARCEL BERLINS, *The Times*

ISBN: 0 00 649830 2

Blood is Dirt

Robert Wilson

Bruce Medway, fixer and debt collector in Benin, West Africa, has heard a few stories in his time. The one that Napier Briggs tells him is patchy but it doesn't exclude the vital fact that two million dollars have gone missing. Bruce is used to imperfect information from clients embarrassed at their own stupidity. But this time it leads to a gruesome death.

It would all have ended there but for Napier's daughter, the sexy, sassy and sussed Selina Aguia, a commodities broker. She launches Bruce into the savage world that her apparently innocuous father had chosen to inhabit – a world of oil and toxic waste scams, of mafia money laundering, of death and violence fuelled by drink, drugs and sex. Worse for Bruce, Selina wants revenge, and with the scam she invents it looks as though she'll get it. But this is a world where blood is dirt – nobody really cares. Not even if they love you.

'For once a novelist influenced by Raymond Chandler is not shown up by the comparison, matching his mentor's descriptive flourishes and screwball dialogue'

Sunday Times

ISBN: 0 00 649975 9

The Dancing Face

Mike Phillips

Museum piece, priceless artefact, spiritual talisman, political bargaining chip – the Dancing Face, a golden mask made for the first great Oba of Benin, means something different to each of those who seek to possess it. But whatever their motivation, such is the lure of the mask that collectors, crooks and politicians alike will stop at nothing – be it murder, kidnapping, blackmail, or espionage – to get their hands on it.

Is it the dark power of the Dancing Face itself that causes sinister events to befall those who come in contact with it? Struggling to understand the source of the mask's power and how best to use it, university lecturer Gus Dixon and his younger brother, Danny, born in Britain of mixed parentage, soon find themselves out of their depth – driven by an idealism that is no match for the ruthless greed of men like corrupt Nigerian exile, Dr Okigbo.

A gripping and original thriller, combining intrigue and action with telling insights into African-European relations and the issue of racial identity.

'This book is brutal, deep, cunning and unbearably beautiful'
Independent

ISBN 0 00 649985 6

The Fig Tree Murder

A Mamur Zapt mystery

Michael Pearce

Why was the body put on the line? Did someone want to halt the progress of the new railway out from Cairo to the 'City of Pleasure' being built in the suburbs? Or was it just another traditional revenge killing?

To answer these questions the Mamur Zapt, British Head of Cairo's Secret Police, has to look both in the luxurious quarters of the dazzling New Heliopolis and in the more humble houses of the dead man's village and in neither place are things quite as straightforward as they seem. What is the significance of the Tree of the Virgins? Does it matter that the gathering place for the Mecca Caravan is only a mile or two away? And what of the ostrich that passed in the night?

'Urbane, intelligent and never patronising, Pearce writes about Egypt with the observant eye of the lover who sees yet forgives all faults'

VAL McDERMID, *Manchester Evening News*

'Effortlessly funny and engaging. Packed, as ever, with fact, flavour and the kind of insouciance which makes history lighter than air'   PHILIP OAKES, *Literary Review*

ISBN: 0 00 649968 6

With Child
Laurie King

San Francisco homicide detective Kate Martinelli is feeling dispirited and rejected after her lover, Lee – who is recovering from a near fatal gunshot wound – decides she needs to spend time on her own. Her only solace is the friendship of bright, quirky, twelve-year-old Jules, who enlists Kate's aid in finding a homeless kid who has gone missing.

When Jules's parents plan a holiday without her, Kate volunteers to take the girl on a visit to the farm where Lee is staying. But events spiral nighmarishly out of control when Jules vanishes from her motel room in an area where a serial killer has been targeting young girls who match her description.

Unbearably gripping and deeply moving, *With Child*, is an extraordinary novel from the award-winning author of *A Grave Talent* and *To Play the Fool*.

'Tense, tortuous and tremendously powerful, this is an emotional rollercoaster ride'   VAL McDERMID

ISBN 0 00 649905 8